Blood of My Brother

<u>By</u>

Zoë and Yusuf T. Woods

RJ Publications, LLC

Newark, New Jersey

RJ Publications
ywoods94@yahoo.com
www.rjpublications.com
Copyright © 2007 by Yusuf T. Woods
All Rights Reserved
ISBN-10: 0978637313
ISBN-13: 9780978637316

Printed in the Canada

September 2007

3 4 5 6 7 8 9 10

Dedications

By Zoë

To my amazing husband Yusuf, your creativity and perspicacity are second to none. This experience has been both a pleasure and an honor, from you I have learned so much. Words alone cannot define all that you are and what you mean to me. I see the genuine passion and growth within you each day, you are my King and I cherish this journey in which we walk together. Thank you for your inspiration, support, love and being a phenomenal husband and father. We love you.

Dedications

By Yusuf

This book is dedicated to my lovely wife Zoë who has been by my side from the start. Baby, if my heart could talk it would speak your name in five different languages followed by these words; I have been looking over my shoulder, keeping my guard up in order to look out for myself for so long that I almost didn't notice that you are here with me always. When I slipped, it was your arms that stopped me from falling and your words of encouragement that turned my rage into ambition after everyone that I loved turned on me. So I thank you and will continue to until the end of time.

Acknowledgements

First and foremost, all praise is due to Allah. Without him I am nothing. This book would not be possible without the help of many people. I would like to give thanks to everyone who took the time to read this book; your support is greatly appreciated. I swear I tried to make each character jump out of the page and walk away and if not this time then maybe the next one, I know I will try. I would like to especially acknowledge and thank Richard Jeanty for this opportunity, for seeing something within my writing and also being understanding when I tried to do too much. Know that it is only me trying to be the best. To my staff at YNZ Productions, I appreciate the push to keep moving the bar.

I would also like to acknowledge Wendell a.k.a. Black from DE (Thank you for being the man you always said you were), Gotti BX, Cooney Fox 60th & Market St., Dough Boys, Prim Rose a.k.a. Primetime, Almeen a.k.a. Lemon Harlem, Hanif Abdulah (A true Don), Dirty Black (The realest person you'll meet), Gizz

HB, Maurice Youmans a.k.a. Mr. Freeze, Lil "E" Montgomery 1st Ave, Lil Cheese Steak (The one who kept it real), Sam a.k.a. Puddy (Long time no see player), Baller (You are still family), Fly (Stop the hating), Big Dog, Jay Hines (It's your turn now, make it do what it do), Claudio Ferrer Jr, Big Scoop, Big Moon (B-more), KB (The Boss), and Scott Hunnewell. R.I.P to the following; Dame, Lil Pittman, Tim Raisen (I cried when you passed), Murder NJ, Abdullah, Balel, Wali, Jahad, Nafisah, Manny Maxxie (You are truly missed).

A very important acknowledgement goes to someone who has had a profound impact on my life, Johnny Brake my late Grandfather. Even when my brother closed your eyes for the last time, you had a smile on your face. I hope that you have one on now as you look over our family. I love you Big Man.

Last but certainly not least my children, you mean the world to me. You are my inspiration every second of my life. Every man in this world will make a mistake but it is the first step that he takes after it that determines whether or not he has learned from it. I am coming straight to you all, I love you. To my mother Beatrice Woods who has made many sacrifices in her life just to balance out the family, if I ever cried a tear it was for the love that you put in my heart, thank you.

Introduction

In the rough streets of Philly, money is like air. You can't live without it, but you can die trying to get it. This book is a high energy drama that puts you right in the middle of the street life. This story could only be told by a person who has lived it. Many have lost themselves by not using the rules that are laid out in this story. The Author introduces us to Roc and his right hand man Boggy. Roc is a boss that makes noise with his hands and not with his mouth as a true Don does.

Together, Roc and Boggy have come a long way. From having their ribs touched due to lack of food, to sitting side by side on a G4 overlooking the Atlantic Ocean. However, it's hard to stay at the top when so many people want your spot. Roc has seen the jealousy, disrespect, and betrayal that come along with being the top dog but the devastating move that comes his way is one that takes things to a new level. What comes out in this story is sure to keep you captivated from beginning to end.

Chapter 1

"Yo, what did I tell you about being on the block? I don't want you on the block, around the corner or down the street from it. Do you hear me?" Roc said as he was talking to his younger brother, Lil Mac. As Lil Mac replied with a small amount of fear in his heart but not noticeable in his voice he said, "yeah, but I wasn't on the block." Roc, with a quick interruption of Lil Mac's sentence, said, "What the fuck you lying to me for when you know that there isn't a soul that walks on that block that I don't know about?" Roc's face tightened as he continued to confront his brother. He was very protective and always wanted Lil Mac to grow up making the right choices and not getting caught up in street life.

Lil Mac looked up to Roc and wanted to be just like him in so many ways. Roc was about 6'3", built at 235 lbs, jet-black hair with deep waves like a bees nest. Along with his one of a kind swagger, his light brown eyes and diesel build, the ladies loved him. The other side of Roc was a cold killer by blood, a man who was in the streets hard and did not want his brother to go in the same direction that he did.

The conversation between Roc and his brother continued as Lil Mac said, "Me and D was on the block looking for his girl." Roc knew that D didn't have a girl but went along with his story anyway, replying, "Oh, that pretty girl I always see D with. I think her brother owes me some money. What's her name?" Lil Mac, now a little speechless did not know how to respond. "Uh, uh huh"…and before he spoke again Roc smacked him in the head, not too hard but just enough to let him know that he'd just been caught in a lie. "For real, I want you to stay off the block. That block is no good, too much shit be jumpin' off and I don't need you out there when something happens or you getting shot," Roc explained. "If that were to go down we'd have to shut down the whole city," Roc said jokingly to put a smile on Lil Mac's face. Lil Mac, still mad that Roc had hit him in the head had fire in his eyes but Roc knew that without a father, sometimes Lil Mac needed to know that it's not a game and it was up to Roc to step up and be head of the house.

Lil Mac responded to Roc's comment about getting shot and said, "Man if I get hit, it's going to be blood everywhere, you feel me? I'm hitting everybody and anybody, if I got to feel pain then I'm going to make sure everybody feels pain, you know what I mean?" It was at that point that Roc knew he was losing his brother to the streets but he was not going to give up on Lil Mac. "Slow down Lil' man…be easy. I need you in school to become that lawyer that you wanted to be. So you can get us a big house, you feel me?" said Roc.

Lil Mac's cell phone began to ring at that moment, "Yo, what up?" he said as he answered it. "Lil Mac, what you doing man?" said D, on the other end of the phone. "I'm here talking to my brother, he's on my back about being on the block last night, so hold on for a minute." As Lil Mac turned to finish talking to Roc, he said, "I feel you, I'll talk to you later Roc…I have to take this call." Lil Mac walked in his room, closing the door so that Roc would not hear his conversation; he got back on the phone to talk to D. "I know we got to get that money but we have to find a new spot to get this shit off. We can't be on his block because that nigga be tripping and if he finds out that I'm pushing work, he will kill me." Lil Mac knew that it would not only make Roc mad if he found out about him selling drugs but Roc would be hurt.

"What about the spot on 13th street where the boy Troy and them be getting money? You know they some cold suckers up there." D was looking out the car window of his old 98' B.M.W that he got from a hustler named Pop. What caught his eye was a girl wearing some tight apple bottom jeans. He wanted to call her over to the car but didn't want to disrespect his main man on the phone during a serious conversation. He replied, "Troy? Oh Okay, the boy that be playing hard, he has the gold Benz? He's the one who had beef with Slick, then gave us money to holla at him so Slick would back off, right?"

Lil Mac answered, "That's the one and they are eatin up there". "All right," D said. "This is what we're going to do, have everybody meet at the house around 7:30 tonight then I can give you the game so that we can get this money". "Nigga, you don't have no game, whatever game you do have is what you took from me," replied D as they both started laughing. D smiled brightly, loving the friendship that he and Lil Mac have. Not too many people can play with Lil Mac at all because of the street respect he wants, just like his older brother Roc. Lil Mac responded to D and said, "Nigga I coach the game. I got more game than a pimp with solid gold boots on. You remember when I stuck up that cat on

51st and Master with a number two pencil? We were on our way home from school and after he gave the money up, I gave the vic the pencil". "I remember that bull shit, that nigga was a real sucker."

"Now that's game, but I'm out...I'll see you later on tonight, one". "All right, one."

They both hung up the phone laughing. Lil Mac turned on the T.V. thinking that soon it would be his turn to have the city on lock and key. Then everybody would know he is not just Roc's Lil Brother, but that he is his own man as well.

Chapter 2

Roc left the brown stone on south 21st street and jumped in his black 4.6 Sports Range Rover with tinted windows. Sitting on 26-inch rims, he rode through North Philly thinking about Lil Mac. Not knowing what he should do to keep Lil Mac away from the streets. Roc was on his way to pick up his main man, Kevin, who lived around the corner from the Eagle's Bar.

Roc, heard his cell phone ring as he was moving along with the traffic. He looked to see who was calling and it was another one of his close friends named Boggy. There was never a time that he needed Boggy and he didn't step up to the plate, guns poppin and all. Roc answered just as the phone stopped ringing and pushed number eight on speed dial to call his top soldier Boggy back.

Boggy answered on the first ring, "Boggy speaking". "Yo what up Boggy, I see you got at me, what's going on?" asked Roc. Boggy replied, "Yeah man, I need you to come by, you know I don't like talking on the phone after the feds got Freddy."

"All right, where you at player?" said Roc, who was starting to feel a headache coming. He knew this wasn't going to be good. Speaking in code, Boggy replied saying, "I'm on block three, in the back. I think I know why that cake is doing the soldier slim and juvenile." "Boggy, I'm about five minutes away but I need you to meet me two blocks over from three because I'm in the Rover and I can't bring this there if I know how you're thinking."

Roc knew that number three and five were coming up slow for the past two weeks. Roc named his blocks by what number he acquired them in. His state of mind went from a cool loving brother to a cold killer with his hand on the 45 caliber revolver he kept in the waistline of his pants. There was no way he was going to let niggas stop the way food was coming to his table. He had his mom and brother to look after. His mind went back to when he was just fifteen years old. His Dad was dead and his mom had just lost her job three weeks before his passing. Now they had nothing to eat and his Mom spent the last of her food stamps. So Roc, whose real name is Odell Miller new that he had to be the man of the house. Roc got his street name when he started rocking people to sleep. But as a kid he always was known as Odell.

Odell remembered going into his father's old room where no one was allowed to go. As he walked in, he could still smell his father like he was right there. He went straight to his father's old shoebox that was all the way at the bottom of the others. The power of his father could be felt; Odell missed and loved him so much. As he pulled out the gun from the box, there was no point where he was afraid of the old 22 handgun that he saw his father use on a man in a bar before. Recalling the incident, Odell was only ten years old at the time. A man named Jeff owed his Dad some money. Jeff was a big man, about 300 lbs and Odell was scared of what the man would do to his father as they started to argue in the bar. His Dad told him to go sit down in the chair by the corner. Before Odell could get to sit down, Jeff took a swing at his Dad, and in one smooth move, his Dad ducked and pulled out his gun. "You're going to give me my money or you're going to take this heat, you dig," said Odell's Dad as he looked Jeff in the eyes. You could see the fear on Jeff's face as he handed over the money to Odell's Dad.

Odell remembered that his Dad's voice played in slow motion as he heard these next words come out of his mouth..."Player please...nobody plays with my money." No sooner then his Dad finished the last word, he heard, Pow! Pow! Pow! And Big Jeff hit the floor after the bullets hit him...these sounds haunted Odell's ears as a kid. Everyone there now had a look of fear on their faces as Odell and his Dad walked out the door together.

When they got in their car, his Dad looked at him with the coolest eyes and said, "Son, never let a man stop you from feeding your family. If you're not man enough to keep what you got, then you're not supposed to have it. That nigga Jeff damn sure wasn't man enough to keep mine and he sure wasn't supposed to have it."

Now, with those words fresh in his head, his Dad's gun in his pocket, the black hoody pulled over his little eyes, he walked down 5th and Brown St. at night in the alley where there were crack heads everywhere.

The cars were back-to-back trying to get some of that Death. Whether it was crack, dope, or power...they had it. Some would kill for it, some would die for it and some, once they got it...would die. Odell walked in the alley listening to people talk. There were two smokers arguing to his right, the tall slim one was wearing a green jacket, dirty brown jeans, and a hat turned to the side of his head. The other person was a short guy with a little size on him, like he used to work out. Speaking to the tall slim guy, he said, "Man, let me get some of that raw so I can get a fresh one up in me." The other person replied, "Come on Fats, you just had your shit and you didn't give me nothing, so you can get the fuck out of here with that."

The tall slim guy was rolling a crack blunt, while drinking his 40 of Old E. Fats stepped up to him ready to take the crack from him and replied, "What the fuck you mean I know you don't think you're not going to give me a fresh one...nigga, you got this fucked up."

"Hold up, Fats, you know I was just playing with you...you...you know I got you, I got you."

"Man, you niggas are going to stop playing all the fucking time, messing with my addiction and shit. Nigga, get a fresh one ready for me."

"Okay man, open this up". Slim passed a new blunt to Fats. Before he saw it coming, Slim was bringing the bottle of Old E. down hard on the top of his head. As Fats was laid out on the ground, Slim yelled out, "That's right, that's right I freshened him right on up," and started dipping down the block.

Odell, still walking slowly, turned his attention to a drug dealer and someone trying to buy something. He heard the conversation as the buyer said, "Come on Vic, I only got seven dollars." She had a smile on her face like she was on the T.V. show Let's Make a Deal. Vic, with his three gold chains on and a Nike sweat suit said, "Bitch, you better go buy a bag of weed and a 40 with those seven dollars. My shit is ten dollars; if you got seven dollars and your head comes with that...then we can work something out."

She said, "Come on Vic, you know I don't like doing that."

"All right then, I'll holla," said Vic as he turned away. "Wait, wait, all right let's go," she said as she and Vic headed to his car.

From the corner of his eye, Odell saw a white man with a black woman sitting in a cream colored Buick. They had to be there from the time he walked up the block. He still would not have seen them if the inside dome light didn't come on. The white man was trying to hide money from the woman, he had it on his left side and she was talking to him with her hand out on the right as she now stood outside the car.

Odell clocked the white man, like a black man in a Chinese store. When he gave the black lady in the red dress two twenty dollar bills she proceeded to walk away. She was a pretty, light skinned woman with her hair falling down her back walking across the street. Her big ass was moving from side to side and then she stopped at Vic's 300 E Benz and knocked on the window while the woman in the car had her head going up and down on Vic's dick.

"Damn, let me roll the window down....don't stop," Vic said to the woman in the car with him as the window was coming down.

"What you want, next or this shit I got in my pocket?" Vic asked the light skinned woman standing outside the car. She replied, "No Vic, I got this sucker and he got money, but he's trying to hold out but I know when I put this ass on him, I'm getting all of that."

"All right, give me a minute," said Vic. The woman outside the car hastily said, Come on Vic, I'm trying to get out of here."

"Yeah, I hear you...so let me put my hand up that dress and play with that thing so I can cum quicker," Vic

21

said to her. As the woman outside the car pulled up her dress a little, she yelled at the woman in the car, saying, "Bitch, handle your BI so I can get this shit off of Vic."

Vic put one finger, then two in her hairy pussy as she stood next to him, stepping up closer to him while he was sitting in the driver's side of his car. While she was doing that, Odell was now right next to the car that she had just gotten out of. With one smooth move, he slid into the back with the gun pointed at the white man's chest. The man's heart is racing nonstop; his eyes are bigger then two fifty-cent pieces.

"Player, give that money up or I'm going to kill you," Demanded Odell. As the white man is passing the money off, he looked at Odell with his blue eyes. He handed over everything he had and Odell said, "Now pull off sucker!"

When the car started, the women in the red dress with Vic, began to holler, "Where you going, baby?"

As his car began to pull off, she only caught part of what he said as he yelled out, "I've been ro…" Just then, those same sounds that haunted Odell before, had blasted off again, Pow! Pow! Pow!

Chapter 3

Lil Mac closed the door to the brown stone on 21st Street. As he walked down the steps, he heard a window open and he looked up to see his mom in the window. She yelled out, "Lil Mac, what did I tell you about leaving this house without saying good-bye and giving me a kiss?" He looked at her pretty smile, chocolate skin with rollers still in her hair. At the age of 53, she looked as though she was only 35.

Lil Mac replied to her, "come on Mom, I'm a man now...don't you think it's time to give that up?"

"Yeah, yeah, I hear you boy, but to me you're always going to be my baby Lil Macky," his mother said as she kept that smile on her face that always soften Lil Mac's heart. He loved her so much but he needed her to see him as a man, just like Roc. Lil Mac blew his mom a kiss and she said, "I knew you wouldn't let an old woman like me down."

As he started walking, he passed Kim sitting on the step. "Girl, what's so funny….I don't see no clowns out here?" Kim was the prettiest girl that Lil Mac had ever seen but she wouldn't give him the time of day. She responded to him saying, "I don't see any men here either, so if you do…let me know."

"Girl, you need to stop playing and get with this boss," Lil Mac said as he proceeded to get into his pearl white Acura. This car was a birthday gift from Roc when Lil Mac turned sixteen. As he drove past the pretty brown stone houses on his way to the hood, he thought about how to get this money to become the next Don. To get himself in the right state of mind to think about work, he slid in the 2 Pac mixed CD that he had made by DJ E. Number eight was his favorite song. There was base through the whole car while he was pushing down hard on the gas and bobbing his head to Pac's words; *I couldn't help but notice your pain...my pain? It runs deep, share it with me. They'll never take me alive I'm gettin' high with my four-five cocked on these suckers, time to die. Even as I was a youngster causin' ruckus on the back of the bus. I was a fool all through high school kickin' up dust, but now I'm labeled as a trouble maker who can you blame?*

24

Lil Mac thought to himself, I have to get this money, its ride or die time. These niggas are acting like I can't get my own money or do my own thing. I know Roc paid for my car, cell phone bill, and everything. But now it is my turn to eat. Matter of fact the next time one of them cats try to play me on the same "little Roc" shit, they can get it wild out in public.

Now that Lil Mac couldn't get money on Roc's block anymore, he had to find a spot to move the 20 ounces of cocaine and the dope that he found in Roc's clothes basket. It has been five weeks and Roc still hasn't said anything about it. Roc did not know it was in there because he never brings drugs in the house. So when he handed the basket to his brother, Lil Mac went through it looking for Roc's Prada shirt and there it was, in the middle of the clothes. Now Lil Mac has money on his mind, and his mind on money.

Lil Mac pulled the car into a parking space behind a burned out Chrysler, Park Avenue with no windows. After sitting on the block for a few hours, he saw the old head, Top Dollar, who used to get big money dealing and running numbers with his dad back in the day. But after the passing of his best friends and partners,

Top Dollar fell back. Now he's dealing hundred dollar packs for Troy just to get by.

Lil Mac let the window down slowly with a smile on his face; he called his old head to the car. "Yo, Top Dollar, let me holla at you, playa." As he started walking toward him, Lil Mac still remembered the times Top Dollar used to come over the house after his Dad passed away.

Top Dollar saw his best friend's son who looked just like his old friend. "What's up, Lil Mac? I see you're still doing it, you dig," said Top Dollar. He talked like he was still in the seventies. "What size shoes you got on this car, fifties?" Top Dollar said laughing.

"Na, something small…get in the car, I need to holla at you on some real shit," replied Lil Mac. Top Dollar got in the car and pushed his seat back to get comfortable and asked, "So, what is the real shit you got on your mind, playa?"

Lil Mac turned to him and answered, "I'm going to keep it real Top Dollar, like I always do. I need this block." "Wow shorty, now you need the block?" Top Dollar responded, laughing and went on to say, "Come on Lil Mac, what you know about this here do or die…you can lose your life and that's real."

26

Top Dollar looked Lil Mac in the eyes, waiting for a reply and saw him with a look that he had seen so many times before.

"I know the kid Troy has five look-outs working on the block, the two kids right there," Lil Mac said as he pointed to the kids that were sitting on the hood of two cars facing each other and continued, "they sit that way so that one can look down the street in one direction and the other could look in the opposite direction. There are two other look-outs parked in a black Volvo down the block with tinted windows. Their seats are laid back, so if you aren't paying attention you wouldn't see them because you can only see the one kid's hat line and the top of the other kid's white T-shirt. He's the one with the AK-47 on his lap. And you my friend…are number five! I know you're selling something on the side for yourself because the fourth house down on the left, the yellow and white one…that is where you sell the crack at. I know every three hours, give or take ten minutes, two cats come to pick up the money, but the move is how they ride around for a half hour making sure nobody is following them just to come back here. I've seen them walk through two yards to put the money in that house right there."

27

Lil Mac pointed to the house in the middle of the block on the opposite side of the street from the crack house. He continued to talk to Top Dollar, "And I bet when I go in there tonight, Troy is going to be in there with my money and that is real."

Top Dollar saw Lil Mac's eyes come back to normal, the same way his father's used to when it was time to put in work. At that moment, Top Dollar knew the kid with his help, would be the next top dog. Not like the sucker Troy that he worked for now. Top Dollar didn't know how many times he told Troy to put the shooter on the roofs and to get the different cars to move the money, but when you're hard headed in this game you have to pay with your money or your life…and sometimes it's both.

As Top Dollar looked at Lil Mac with a smile on his face, he said, "Is it just me and you or do we have some back up?" "It's just me and you," Lil Mac said, joking with Top Dollar to see what the O.G. would say. Lil Mac was holding back a smile, trying hard not to laugh just as Top Dollar said, "Lil Mac, my shot is not like it used to be but it's only four people in the house with the money and I know with my 45, I can hit maybe three. So you're going to have to shoot one or two."

Lil Mac stopped him as he finished his sentence, "I was just playing, I got a team but I want you right by my side when we do this tonight because you're Top Dollar. Ain't no sucker going to have my Dad's partner selling no packs for some jeans and sneakers. It's time for you to shine again, you with me?"

"To the end, you're my partner's seed and I know he's looking down smiling at a player. Some people just know how to shine, but once you've mastered that, you control the whole light and I am going to give you the whole light, I'm too old for it now."

Lil Mac looked at the clock, it read 6:53pm. "All right Mr. G.E., turn my song up." Top Dollar turned up the music and asked, "Is this the only song this car plays?" After hearing the song eleven times now since he'd gotten into the car, he started to memorize it. "Yeah, that's the only song it plays...you got a problem with that?" replied Lil Mac.

Top Dollar started singing as they pulled off, "They'll never take me alive, I'm getting high with my 45." They both started laughing.

Chapter 4

Bang…Bang…Bang, was the sound that brought Roc back to reality as Boggy knocked on his window as he sat parked on 7th and York Streets. Roc didn't know how long Boggy was standing there.

"Roc, open the damn door!" Boggy demanded as he grinned and pulled the door handle. Boggy was dressed in his green and brown camouflage army suit with brown wheat Timbs. He also had on his Platinum chain with Ride or Die on it that matched the iced out watch on his right hand. Boggy was about 5'10", 285lbs. Muscular build, brown skin with a low hair cut.

"Man, you all right? You look like you were in another world," said Boggy as he slowly closed the door after getting into the Range. He looked down at his feet making sure that he didn't put any marks on his Timbs. "Yeah I'm cool, what up, pretty boy?" replied Roc as they hit hands for their special handshake and then he asked, "So what's up with the money slowing up on blocks three and five?" "Come and jump in my ride, I got to show you this shit," Boggy said.

On the way to Boggy's Maxima, Roc thought he saw his brother Lil Mac rode by. "Yo, is that Lil Mac's car right there?" Roc said as he pointed at an Acura and then continued, "Hey that is him, and he's with that old head that hustle's for that boy Troy we got on 13th Street." He called out to Top Dollar as he put on his seat belt. Roc had been in four accidents while Boggy was driving and two hit and runs.

"Yeah, that's his name, what the fuck he doing with him?" Roc said, talking to Boggy. "Man, I don't know, probably just giving him a ride," replied Boggy. He really wanted to tell Roc that he knew Lil Mac was selling drugs but he knew it would hurt his best friend's heart. Roc wanted so much for Lil Mac to finish school and go on to college so that he could make it in this world and get out of this place that only brought death.

"Yeah, I went at him, he tried to lie to me and all. I know I'm going to have to stay up on him and the summer just started." Boggy pulled the car over to the corner of block three. As soon as the car came to a stop, two men were at the driver side window. The one with his hand on his 45mm under his jacket knocked on the tinted window. When it came down, he handed Boggy the two guns he always held for him. Both of the men that approached were Boggy's personal shooters. They had two cars, a place to stay and mad guns. The walkie talkies that they had in their cars were so that Boggy could reach them at anytime and vise versa.

The relationship between Boggy and his shooters, Bo and Chris, started back in the day. Bo and Chris were putting mad work in on the stick up tip. They would get the drug dealer, keep the money and sell the work to Roc for a low price. Then they started to get high so they were sticking up everybody and anybody. One day they robbed a Rite Aid and got locked up. Roc got word and bailed them out. When they made it out of jail, Roc asked them if they wanted to make some real money again and they answered yes. Roc put them in a rehabilitation center. After they finished, Roc and Boggy showed them how to really shoot a gun. The way the government trains, like how to shoot on the move with one hand, how to shoot with one eye in the rain and a lot of other things that they needed to know to become warriors. Now that they were getting money with Roc over the years, and have been through so much together, they would die for Roc and Boggy. They knew that the feeling was mutual.

Bo and Chris didn't see Roc until he started to get out the car. Chris was the slim one with a light blue Pelle Pelle jacket on. When he saw Roc, he started smiling and said, "There goes my player right there. What's the deal, boss man? I hit you up last night…that girl was out here looking for you again. I hear she was over ten and six before she came here. She said she wasn't getting off the block until she saw you. I was ready to put one of these hot balls in that pretty ass."

Chris showed his gun that was under his shirt. He continued talking to Roc saying, "But she asked for you. If she would have asked for Boggy, she would be right behind J hood's house because Boggy is just like me…if a bitch is out of line, she get it too."

They all started laughing as they walked behind Boggy to go where ever it was that he was taking them. "Yeah, I got your message dawg. I don't know what's up with that girl. Next time hit her up," Roc said with a smile. Chris knew that Roc was just joking because Roc only killed when it was necessary. Roc explained, "She knows that I have a wife and I'm trying to open the club in a month or two. I don't have time for her shit. You know what's really funny…I don't even know the freak's name."

They were all still laughing as Boggy came to a stop and said, "Yo Roc, look right there at the house with the three people coming out of it. That is why number three and five are coming in slower then usual. There go four more people. See, they think they're slick since our blocks are four blocks apart from each other they come sit in the middle. That house is where the lady Rose cooks our work up at. You know, Rose…the one with the good head. I don't think it's her work but I still don't know whose it is yet. I sent a couple smokers up there to cop and they got some nice work, but I needed to know what you wanted to do before I put an end to this shit."

Anger was all over Boggy's face as he watched more people come out of the house. "Roc, you want me to go in there and shut this bitch down, cause can't nobody get money on this side of town but you," said Chris.

"Take it easy main man. I see the little work they're trying to get off, but we don't know enough about them yet to have mighty whitey zipping up body bags around here. Now, it could just be Ms. Rose trying to get off some of that stuff she gets for cooking up for niggas. This is what I want you to do," continued Roc, "Get the bulls, Mohammed and Shamone up here to watch the

34

house for a few days to see who's dropping the work off and where the rest of the heads are, because you must kill the head for the body to fall."

Roc knew as soon as he said it that it was the wrong move. That he should burn the house to the ground just for the disrespect of them trying to sell in a 5 mile radius. At that moment, Roc knew he wasn't going to be in the game much longer. The feeling has been coming but now seeing how much his brother wanted to be like him made him realize that he had to stop before Lil Mac wanted in the game. As soon as the club is up and running, Boggy can have this if it's not too late, thought Roc as he walked back to the car.

"They on their way Roc", Chris said after he finished relaying the message sent from Roc to Mohammed and Shamone. "What we getting into tonight?" added Chris. "Man I don't know, why don't you call the bull and see if he's staying in M.I.A. or coming back. If he is coming back, you know we're in for two days putting this shipment together," said Roc. Back on the block, Boggy passed the two guns back to Chris but kept his glock 10 in the back of his pants. "Come on, you know I got to call him from a pay phone. Not on the block though, I need to see if all the pick ups went through," said Boggy, "Let's roll. When was the last time you did a pick up?"

"I don't know, it has been a minute," answered Roc as he cocked the 9mm back.

Roc said, "Damn, its 7:30 all ready!" Boggy answered, "Yeah, and if the bull isn't coming back tonight, I got to change and put this hoopty up and jump in the Benz or my baby the M.4. You know we're putting that party together for your young bull that caught the case three years ago."

"M. Easy?" asked Roc. "Yeah," answered Boggy.

"That's tonight? I don't know what's been up with me...That's my little man," said Roc. "I know that's why we did it big for him. I know your mind has been all over the place these past few weeks. You still haven't found that work or the dope yet did you?" asked Boggy

Roc just shook his head, knowing he had never lost work in his life until now.

"Man...that is not like you at all. I hope all this money is not starting to make you soft because I need the old Roc back. The Roc I helped get away when you had that old rusty gun, smoking in your hand after you shot that white man. The way that you jumped out of the car and ran down the block, I knew you didn't know where you were going, but you didn't care, you needed the money to feed your family and I saw it in your eyes. That's why I let you run up in my house to get away from that cop on your ass. I know you're trying to open the club and a whole lot of other things. So, take some time for yourself and I'll hold it down," said Boggy.

Roc thought this might be the best time to tell Boggy that after this shipment, he was out of the game. He didn't need anymore money. Roc was sitting on a few million from his ten year run. Now it was time to put the gun down and get his family out of Philly, and take Boggy with him if he wanted to go. It just seemed as though right now was not the time to tell him.

Roc responded to what Boggy said to him, "Yeah, I think I'll do that, get out of town for a few days. So if the work comes back tonight, put it up until tomorrow and you can take care of that. My nigga M. Easy, that's my heart, that nigga is wild as shit and when he touch down, have our people right there. I'm not going to miss the homecoming for the world and I'm going to be on break from now until the end of next week. Take me to my ride so that I can get ready."

"That's right, do you playa. And when you're ready, have a limousine pick you up," said Boggy. "That's right, you know how I do" replied Roc. I'm going to pick up M. Easy in a limo and take him to his party too. I know his people already went to get him from Western. I got him a car last week with the T.V., rims and the whole nine."

Roc pulled away from the sidewalk into the street, knowing that he was out of the game and was going to take a trip to Japan. When he got back he'd hoped to be ready to tell them, if only it were that easy.

"Now this is the last time I'm going to go over this shit...we ride ruff and handle this nigga Troy, he's sweet as bear meat. But the bull O.J pops that heat. That is why I want you, D, and your team on the block by the crack house. Be on him before we hit the house with the money. As soon as we go in, hit him off with the R.I.P. Top Dollar, you, black, and catty," Lil Mac said as he was pointing at Black who was a really dark skinned guy wearing a black sweat suit which made it difficult for anyone to see him at night. Catty was sitting right next to him and had on the same gear as did the rest of the team.

Lil Mac continued to give instructions, "Top Dollar, for the tenth time...I need you to get the two dudes in the first car. Me, K.B., and Nay Nay are going in the money house from the back so we will not be on the block all at once. That means Corn, you and Raw have the guys sitting on the cars first because everybody has to hit their spot at the same time. Put your walkie talkie on channel 8 and your watch on 10:00pm. Now that gives us one hour before show time...any questions?"

"Yeah, we're not going in there on some, put your hands up shit...we're going in there popping shit, right?" asked Nay Nay. She had green eyes; caramel skin and a short hair cut like one of the boys but she was as pretty as Jada Pinkett in the movie "Set it off."

"Listen Nay Nay...we're not trying to have anybody on us, we're money getters so it's all about the money. But when we say nobody move and a nigga move...put him on his back, anybody else?" Lil Mac asked. Nobody opened their mouth. You could hear a pin drop in the silence. "So let's get this money!" He added.

They jumped in five cars, three people in each and it took them about a half an hour to make it to 13th street. It took 15 minutes for them to get into place. Lil Mac picked up his black walkie talkie with the neon light on 8 and started the show. "We on in ten, D where you at?" Lil Mac asked. "Five houses up from the crack spot, walking slowly. Yo, it's only one dude on the car in the middle of the block" replied D.

Conversation between Top Dollar and Lil Mac;

"Top Dollar, you hear that?" asked Lil Mac, talking into his earpiece.

"Yeah, I know I got Sam already. I caught the sucker taking a pee as we were coming through the alley. I put him in the trunk, you dig?" said Top Dollar

"Yeah, I dig player," answered Lil Mac.

"Black, you get that? It's one on one now, you and Corn can Back D up."

"Roger," replied Black. "Nigga, we're not fifty, so cut that bull shit out! Five minutes...everybody in their places," ordered Lil Mac. Smoothly, everyone moved into place.

Chapter 5

"Roll the fucking dice nigga...your point little Joe. I killed that nigga last week and he had seven bitches with him and here they come right now. Seven," Troy said as he hollered at the big man on the floor who was sweating like someone poured water all over him. Troy's a tall slim man, about 6'3" tall with the heart of a cat but when you're making money and can pay people on the low to have your back like Roc, he could talk tough. "Nigga, I'm going to hit this four in the door and then I'm coming with seven, bitch!" replied the big man. "Then step your bet up you flea as nigga," Troy demanded. "Ok put two more g's on the 10 and 4." "Bet!" Before the dice hit the wall, the door flew off the hinges.

"Nobody move!" Nay Nay had her gun on the two men that were sitting at the table. KB slid by her with his gun on the fat guy and Troy while Lil Mac started going through the house to see if anymore people were there. Lil Mac went down stairs first and then upstairs looking into each room like a pro. You would never have known that this was his first stick up for some real money. But Lil Mac knew he was in the big leagues now and there was no turning back. Lil Mac heard a shot and came running down the stairs to see the fat guy's brain on the wall and his body lying on the floor.

"What the fuck happened," he asked. But he sounded funny since his mask was over his mouth. "The fat nigga moved so I popped him," said Nay Nay. Lil Mac walked over to Troy. "We can do this any way you want, the hard way or the harder way. Since your man's brain's splattered on the wall...I suggest you think carefully about it. Now that shit's funny," Lil Mac said with obvious sarcasm in his voice. He continued talking to Troy, "So, I'm going to start by telling you what I know. For one I know that this is the money house, two...that money doesn't leave here until twelve o'clock, I'm pretty good at this game. But the game is over so off the money or I'm going to off you." Lil Mac slowly raised the 9mm to Troy's head then cocked it back. Troy's heart beat faster than an Amtrak train. He was so scared that Lil Mac only had to ask once.

Troy replied, "The money is in the safe that's in the wall. The combination is 0-2-32-4-33." Just like that, they were looking at $250,000. Troy was kicking himself because the safe was only supposed to have $70,000 in it but he had been so laid back that he was taking the money every two days instead of every five hours like he was supposed to.

"Put your face against the wall! Yeah, ya'll nigga's been eating for too long…it's time for me to get money, pussies," D hollered in the mad face of O.J. while the rest of his team was tying the last few people up in the house. "Nigga you know you got to kill me. Fuck that mask you got on. I got the keys to the city so I'll find out who you are and I'm not going to stop until I get you," said O.J.

"You must not be able to hear too well because I told you who I was. 'Get Money Click' nigga! I'm the second gun," D said this loud enough so that the rest of the dudes in the house could hear him. Then he pulled the trigger and smiled as O.J.'s head popped back before he hit the floor. "Where the rest of the butter at? and I mean, tell me right now or they will be putting 'Get money did this' on your head stone." The slim man on the floor could not stop talking. He started telling about

43

where the gun was in the cellar and everything. After they had gotten the gun, two half bricks of cocaine, and a brick of dope they were ready to go.

"This is get money 2 to get money 1, we're ready on your go," D said speaking into his walkie talkie, hoping everything went right. A response came back saying, "This is get money 1, we'll be ready in ten, so move out in ten." "OK," D replied.

Lil Mac walked up to Troy looking him straight in the eyes and said, "Feel this, you had a nice run but this is my block now. I don't want to see anybody but 'Get Money' getting money here. If I ever see you or any of your suckas on this block again, I'm going to get your mom who lives up in Summerville, your baby's mom that lives on the small block by the store in Nice Town, and then I'm going to kill your bitch ass! Do you understand me?"

Troy, scared and crying answered, "Man….I will never come on this block again. I don't want any part of this, I just want to go home please…please let me go." He knew that this was not his last time running the block but he just wanted to make it out of there to fight another day.

In no time, Lil Mac, Top Dollar, and D had the block doing almost double the numbers that Troy was doing with Get Money pushing crack and dope. Top Dollar was put in charge of making the block safer so that no one could take it back. Lil Mac sat at the head of the table at a smoker's house that Top Dollar put on the payroll like many others. Top Dollar made so many moves so it would be hard to keep track of them. They never met for business in the same place twice within three months.

Looking at all the money on the table, Lil Mac knew this was only the beginning. He had his own team now and their names would be ringing all over the city. Thinking about how to get this money without his brother finding out until it was time, was the hard part. Lil Mac gave everybody their share of the money made for the week and said, "This has been another Get Money meeting and it's only right that we get money. These first few weeks are just the beginning. In a minute, the city will have no choice but to talk about us. Once the streets start talking, niggas listen. It is because of that, I am changing my name. When we are in the streets my name is still Lil Mac but when it comes to this Get Money shit, call me 'Solo'. Now is not the time for me and Roc to be going at it. A lot of money in the city is going to start slowing up and the holidays aren't going to be the same this year for any hustler. I don't care if a nigga is selling socks, we're on him."

The reason for Lil Mac changing his name was because he wanted to take every possible precaution to prevent Roc from finding out he was all in now. Roc would kill him and Lil Mac wasn't trying to die, so he definitely wasn't going out without a fight.

Chapter 6

Two months had passed and Roc still had not taken his vacation. There was too much going on with the club, the block, and this new team on the street. Roc didn't know where they came from. First it was said that Ms. Rosie was selling the work for the 'Get Money' team. In the beginning, Rosie wasn't getting any real money. Now there were runners and look outs. They had the whole block doing numbers. Roc was trying to find out who the head man was. He knew that if he killed the head, the body would follow.

Then there was the issue of Lil Mac moving out of the house. This hurt Roc but they still played ball together every Sunday morning. Roc was proud of Lil Mac becoming a man with his own apartment and new job working in the store on 13th street. Roc just didn't like where it was located but it was a job and it kept Lil Mac off the street. So every time Roc wanted to see Lil

Mac, he would go buy some shoes or a leather jacket so that they could talk like old times.

The Sun had just gone down as the night slowly came in. Roc knew the time had come to do what had to be done, even if he didn't want to. As he sat at the head of the table with Boggy at the other end, there was not a smile at the table of thirty or more top men from Roc's team. M. Easy began saying, "These niggas are getting out of hand, Roc. There is no way in hell I'm going to go home and have niggas on the corner of my block hollering 'Get Money' like they live there. Roc, I know that you said to let them ride until we find out who they run for. So I asked them on some real cool shit to take that down the street because I can't let nobody sell drugs where my family lives, especially having my mom there. Do you know what these kids said to me? And yes, I said kids…these niggas are actually kids to me." The voice of M. Easy became louder and the pain on his face was evident.

He continued his story and went on to say, "this kid told me 'Get Money' is getting money here now! Where I live, I'm looking at this nigga like; he got to be crazy to talk to me like that. He actually looked me in the face and said this shit like I'm a cold sucker. I had my hands in my hoody and a gun in both hands, so I hit him first….Boom, then his man, Boom-Boom. Get money with that devil now nigga!

I called Boggy to bring the van so that we could take the bodies off the block. Roc you know I just came home and I'm on some 'feed my family and lay back shit.' But I will die before I let one of these nobody ass niggas disrespect me."

Roc knew about the story before he called the meeting. That's why there were so many people called to the meeting instead of an assault war. It would be just the top ten usually, and they would give the orders to the rest of the people. Roc felt that nothing but blood was going to fill the streets. Some of the faces he was looking at may not be seen again. There was no way he would let his team go to war and not be on the front line.

After hearing the story, he called his team of young guns from out of town. These three men had been in war with Roc four times and they do their best work when the situation calls for kill or be killed. Roc met them on block 4. They used to come down to buy work from Coatesville, Pa. This is a small town about 45 minutes from Philly. In a place like this, cats get money like they are in the city, off the cocaine business.

The head of these three was a guy named Manny. He never talked around people he didn't know. He thought 24-7, trying to figure out the next mans move. There weren't too many people he trusted in this game of life or death. The ones he trusted were Roc, Boggy, and his two main men, Raja and Buff.

Raja was the hot tempered one, if he thought something was wrong, he popped the gun first and then let them ask the question. At 240 lbs and in good shape, not too many people could keep him cool but Manny. His 6'0" frame, brown skin and bald head helped him get the girls when he wasn't killing people.

The biggest problem in the crew was big Buff. He weighed about 320 lbs standing at 5'11". Big Buff was too fat to do runs, plus he couldn't fight. So he started popping his gun at an early age. A person can only take so many ass beatings in their lifetime.

The three of them were standing on the block talking to Roc and Boggy, waiting on the runner to bring the three kilos. A black ford wagon with tinted windows slowly rode up the block. Raja saw it first because he was always looking for something to go wrong. When the window of the wagon started to come down, Raja was already walking passed it. Before the first gun made it out of the window, he had already given the heads up to the rest of the crew that was standing on the corner.

As Raja started firing on the side of the wagon, Manny had his guns out in half of a second and started firing into the front. Buff moved out from the back of a parked car into the street behind the wagon and began shooting with a gun in both hands. When the shooting stopped, the wagon had more holes in it than Tiger Woods dropped. Roc kept his gun in his hand as he ran up to the car to see if these were the guys he just had words with in a club two days ago.

Roc had then realized that Buff, Manny, and Raja moved like the A-Team. So, for the favor of saving his life, Roc gave them the three kilos and every time he needed some real work put in, he would pay them.

Now, they stood behind Roc as he said to M. Easy, "I feel your pain because if you feel pain, then everyone in this room does and personally...I don't like pain. I bring it, so now it's time to see if the 'get money kids' know how to get blood. Mohammed and Shamone, you've been watching the block Rosie started, right?" They both answered, "Yeah."

Roc continued, "Now, I want you to shut it down and get your teams ready, but leave some room for four people because I need some work. I looked at the note you wrote on her block and it seems to me, that 8 o'clock would be the best time, is that right?" They answered, "Between 8 and 11 o'clock would be the best time."

"So 9 o'clock it is. Boggy, I need you to hold it down here and beef up the guns on our blocks because I have a war to finish and they don't even know it has started," said Roc.

Chapter 7

The night wasn't too dark on Rosie's block because of the street lights and the traffic that traveled through there to cop drugs. With the extra lights, they still didn't see Roc's team in the middle of the block.

Mohammed had his team at the top spread out; four people in one van with six people on foot. They had on old clothes to look as if they were junkies ready to buy some drugs. Mohammed was wearing an old dirty Eagles hoody sweatshirt over his bullet proof vest. His black sweat pants smelled of beer and urine.

Shamone was at the end of the block with his team of ten. He couldn't wait to get it started at two minutes before nine. It only took them a half an hour to get into position. From Shamone's knowledge of the block, he knew the Get Money click wasn't ready for this war they were about to get.

Roc tuned on his walkie talkie and said, "30 second count down" as Manny was walking up the steps to the house where the crack was sold. Buff at the same time, slid into the side door of the building. With his black and green camouflage outfit on, gun in both hands, Raja walked into the front door when two dudes came walking out. Raja heard Roc say go and then let the first man on his left have it in the neck. His second shot hit the man in the chest. The shot killed the man before he'd hit the floor. Roc hit the other man in the head first and once the man had fallen to the ground, Roc hit him two more times to make sure he was dead.

"Yo, you hear that?" said Shorty as he paused his Play Station game. Shorty was one of the men in the crack house. Another man with him named Low replied, "I don't hear shit, push play and get this ass beatin." Another man was in the kitchen bagging up the crack when the door came crashing in. That's when Manny, with a gun in each hand, started firing. A slug hit the man, knocking him out of his chair as he sat at the table. Manny turned his black 45 back and forth while saying, "Nobody move!"

Manny couldn't see the two men in the living room. A voice said, "Oh shit," it came from Shorty as he and Low went for their guns that were on the couch. Shorty had his gun in hand when the front door came crashing in. Raja was standing on top of it as Shorty had the drop on him. Shorty turned around so that he could level the gun on Raja's chest. Just then, three shots came through the front window and one hit Shorty dead in the back of his head. The other two hit him in the back.

As Low put his hands up, nobody in the kitchen turned around. They were too scared after seeing their man U-God die in front of them. Raja ran up on Low, put his gun to Low's head and said, "You thought you had me nigga, didn't you? It's a shame your last thought was wrong!" Boom! Boom…echoed through the room as pieces of Low's brain went flying. "Yo Roc, what you want me to do with these two clowns, off them and get the work?" Raja asked. "No, just get the drugs and the money they are coming with us, Roc replied.

Shamone and three of his team members had the people in the money house on the floor with their hands tied behind their backs, while the rest of the team had the people that worked the block up against the wall, as they were going through their pockets and patting them down. The two men standing side by side tried to run but didn't make it passed the first parked car before shots rang out. The bigger man was hit four times in the back and twice in the head while the second one was hit a lot worse by bullets from David's gray Tech 9mm that held sixty-four in a clip. More than half of those bullets hit the second guy who'd tried to run away. David shouted out, "Who wants to run now?"

At the top of the block, Mohammed had killed four people and was now shooting at the fifth, who was trying to make it to his car. Mohammed's team had the whole top of the block on lock and key. From the second Roc said go, Mohammed moved like a cold killer; giving orders to his team while at the same time putting his gun to work.

Three men ran from the back of a house when one of the vans pulled up and people started jumping out with guns in their hands. Mohammed wasn't in the van; he was on the ground with a smile on his face. For this short moment, he was back in the war in Iraq. When the three took flight, two of them went in the same direction running down the street. The other one ran up the block. Mohammed was on his feet in seconds, letting off shots while running.

On the opposite side of the street, a man was shot in the back by Mohammed as he continued running down the block, not stopping to see if the man was dead. Mohammed jumped on top of a car to get a better look at two men that were crossing the street and then lit off four more shots at them. Both men were hit by the bullets and fell to the ground.

Out of the corner of his eye, Mohammed saw a brown skin dude running beside a house probably trying to get to the next block. The man never made it since he was hit by Mohammed's first shot in the leg which put him face down in the grass. Mohammed walked up on him and turned him over so that he could see the man's face. "You may wear the same uniform as I sir, but you are not my brother. Allah Akbar," screamed Mohammed who was coming out of his war flashback after putting two shots in the man's face. He walked out from beside the house to see that nobody was moving on the whole block except for their crew.

As the people on the wall were getting naked, one tried to make it to his car by acting as if he were part of Roc's crew. The kid walked with confidence, like he was on the winning side. Nobody paid him any attention until his interior car light came on. That's when Mohammed walked up on him and asked, "Are we going somewhere?" as a shot knocked off a piece of the guys head.

Roc, Boggy, Manny Raja, and Buff stood in a circle with Dan who is about six feet tall, 260 lbs and had blood running down his face from the blunts that Buff would smoke and then touch Dan's face with it burning him. Then his partner Veg would get it in the eyes. They had all been in the basement for over two hours trying to beat the identity of their leader out of them. The first hour, Manny and Boggy were taking turns knocking Veg and Dan out.

Now, Roc wanted a name. It was dark in the basement because there were no windows, just concrete walls and floors. The one light was hanging in the middle of the room, right in front of their face.

"Wake the fuck up!" demanded Roc as he poured cold water on Dan and Veg's faces. As they came back to reality, Buff back handed them as Roc said, "now you're going to give me the name of the man running ya'll shit and where his head rests...or you can get this." Roc moved his black 45mm in his right hand putting his finger on the trigger and continued, "It's going to go straight through the front of your skull." Then, Roc put the 45mm to Veg's head and said, "So start talking."

Veg could hardly talk because he was frightened by the cold steel that was touching his face and stuttered as he said to Roc, "Ok...Ok...hhhis name is Solo and that's all I know. I never met him or saw him before. If I knew where he lived, I would tell you...that's my word, on my kids."

"Are you sure?" asked Roc. "I'm sure," Veg replied. Roc pulled the trigger and Veg fell over onto the floor. Dan started to pee himself. His eyes got so big that one would have thought he'd just had a hit of crack.

"That's not good enough," said Roc. Then he put the hot gun to Dan's face. Dan began to scream in pain and the blood on his face made it hard for him to see. Raja picked him up. Dan did not want to die, so he started to talk.

"Veg told you right, his name is Solo and not too many people have ever seen him. I don't even know what he looks like, but I know he has a store on 13th street. Not where they sell the drugs but on the other side where the white people shop. I don't know the name of the street but they have a Giant and stuff, you know where it's at, the store called Philly Raw."

Roc was at a loss for words because of what he had just heard. He made a war on this man named Solo that he knew nothing about. But the man was so close to his family. Roc didn't know what to think. All that he knew was that he had to get in touch with Lil Mac and make sure he was all right. Roc didn't know what he would do with himself if something happened to Lil Mac.

Roc picked up his cell phone and called Lil Mac. His brother answered on the second ring. "Yo, what's up?" Roc felt like the weight of the world was lifted off of his shoulders when he heard Lil Mac's voice. He answered, "Yo Mac, I'm calling to make sure you're coming to play ball tomorrow because I need to talk to you and its really important. So, if you have anything else to do, put that shit to the side because I need to holla at you."

Lil Mac said, "Roc I'll be there and you're not going to win the game this time. Yo Roc somebody is at my door so I will see you tomorrow…one." Roc gave Buff the head nod. This was the sign to put Dan out of this life and into the next. Buff pulled the trigger of his 9mm as the sound echoed through the basement. Roc walked up the old steps thinking about how he was going to tell Lil Mac he had to give up his first job because of him. Roc knew that whoever this guy named Solo was, he would hit back. He just wasn't sure when and how hard.

Roc had been watching how the Get Money click was making money. The way they were taking over blocks that didn't have any real power, just a couple cats here and there selling drugs but nothing big. Roc knew that if he didn't put a stop to them selling on his side of town, they would try to take over more than just one block.

As Roc walked out the old row house to go down the street to his old Buick with tinted windows, he didn't see the eyes that were watching him when he pulled out into the road. "There goes our man right there," said a fat man with a 45mm on his waist as he spoke to another man and began to follow Roc.

Chapter 8

Lil Mac woke up with a terrible headache from the news that he'd received from D after he had last spoken with Roc. He answered his door to find D standing there with his face red and eyes wet like he had been crying. He walked right passed Lil Mac into the front room and started pacing back and forth. "D what's going on dawg, are you all right?" asked Lil Mac with a look of concern for his best friend. "Yo, them niggas done killed Catty man," D said as he broke down in tears. Trying to pull him self together so that he could tell Lil Mac the news he said, "Shot him…in the back of the head then just left him there," he said

"Left him where? Who did this?" Lil Mac was in shock, not fully understanding what had just happened. "Man, we were on Rosie's block picking up the money from the house when them suckers ran up in there. They killed a lot of us but why Catty? He never did anything to anybody. Man this is war, we can't let this go," D shouted, mad and upset.

D took a seat in the chair that was in the corner and wiped the tears off of his face before he started to talk again. "Those niggas raped the whole block, and then they took Veg and Dan."

After listening to the story, Lil Mac didn't know what he felt more, pain from the death of his men or the pain from the disrespect. "What the fuck were they doing on Rosie's block anyway?" asked Lil Mac as he walked up to D and looked him in the eyes. If they weren't best friends, Lil Mac would have killed him right there in the chair. Lil Mac told D when they first started giving Rosie work for cooking up for them and it was going so fast, that she would need to buy an ounce every three hours.

Lil Mac saw the look in D's eyes when she asked them to put some work on the block one night when she was cooking up for them. Lil Mac said "no" about ten times because he knew that was Roc's side of town and Roc would not have it. As Lil Mac talked, a tear ran down his face but not for the men that he'd just lost. The tear was for the fact that he had just been pushed into a war with one of the few people that he loved.

"I told you not to put anything on that block, not anything. What the fuck is wrong with you...you're hard headed!" Lil Mac yelled. "No man, it wasn't even like that, the money started coming so fast. I gave her an ounce one day and then it was two, the next thing I knew she was making $20,000 a week. When the money was on the table, it was cool right?" replied D. But before he finished talking, Lil Mac had his gun pointed in D's face.

"Nigga, don't you ever play with me. You need to die because you killed my men. You killed Catty over some money. We're making over $300,000 every two weeks and that's going up, but you wanted more," Lil Mac said. D had never seen Mac this mad in his life. He knew that he was wrong and that his actions got Catty and the other men killed. So if Mac didn't kill him, he would do anything in his power to see that whoever did this died.

Lil Mac put the gun down to his side and said, "From now on, you take your orders from Top Dollar. I don't even want to talk to you. Tell Top Dollar to have everybody at the spot at eight tonight. Now get the fuck out of my face."

Walking to his black B.M.W. Lil Mac forgot that he could not let Roc see him in that car so he had to take his Acura. On the way to see Roc, so many thoughts were going through Lil Mac's head. He wondered if Roc knew that he was the head of the Get Money click, was this a set up, if he did know…what would he do? Lil Mac wasn't sure if he should have brought his gun.

Pulling up to the park, he saw Roc shooting the ball and hitting all net. When Roc saw him, a big smile shined across his face. As Lil Mac walked on the court Roc said, "What's up big man, you all right? You look like something's wrong in your life. You know I'm here, what's the deal?"

"Nah, I'm cool. Check the ball up," responded Lil Mac. "Hold up, I'll school you in a minute but I need to holla at you first," said Roc. They walked over to the table and sat down and he began to talk, "You're a man now and I respect you as one. Something went down between me and that cat Solo you work for at the store." Lil Mac almost fell off the table when he heard his alias come out of Roc's mouth.

"So I need you to stop working there for a minute. Just until I handle this situation. I can't have anything happening to you," explained Roc. "Come on Roc, you just said that I'm a man now. Then you came at me on some kid shit like I can't take care of myself. I'm getting sick of it and I'm not quitting my job. I don't have no beef with Solo. You got to worry about Solo; I don't even know him and never heard of him. Whoever told you that he owns Philly Raw, lied to you because Mr. Brown owns it and he is at least fifty years old," Lil Mac said.

Roc looked at Lil Mac intently and replied, "Where did all of this hard core stuff that you've been into come from? I'm just trying to look out for you and that you're going to work shit is out the window. If I say you're not going to work, that's it. You're not going!"

"See that is why I left the house and went solo, it must kill you to see me doing my own thing. Even when we were growing up, Roc, you wouldn't let me fight my own battles. I told you I could beat Robby and you would not let me fight him. So we didn't fight because you were there. But you weren't there to stop him from messing with me the next time. When I broke his back he was in a wheel chair for months. You still wouldn't let me become my own person...I'm not just Roc's little brother. On the real, I don't know if I will make it in this cold world. But in the end, we'll see." Lil Mac had just told Roc a lot of what he had wanted to say for a long time.

"I'm not trying to hear that shit, you and Mommy are all we have and I'm not going to let anything happen to you," Roc insisted as he put his hand on Lil Mac's shoulder. "Man, get your hands off of me, I ain't no sucker," said Lil Mac as he pushed Roc's hand off him. "You should have thought about that before you started killing people," Lil Mac shouted as he started to walk to his car. Roc could not believe his ears. He froze, just watching his brother walk away and then pull off in his car. All Roc could think about is how Lil Mac may have known about the body. He never let Mac know about that part of the game. With the look that Lil Mac gave Roc, if looks could kill he would be dead. The way that Lil Mac acted and the things that came out of his mouth were very unlike him. But it was the look from Lil Mac that Roc just could not get out of his head.

The men that were still following Roc were still watching him and had just written down Lil Mac's license plate number. They were watching the drug trades in Philly along with the D.E.A. for the last three years trying to get Roc and Boggy. These two cops were out of the 39th Station. Detective Josh Rayfield was a big man but he didn't have the muscles he had ten years prior. Now he was fat from sitting around on all of the late night stakeouts like that one. His gray hair and the glasses he wore made him look older than the 43 years that he'd lived. His partner for the last six years is a man by the name of Michael Johnson.

Michael wanted to work for the F.B.I. so desperately that if it were possible to not sleep so that it would happen faster, he would find a way to do it. The two are an odd couple. Michael has blond hair and blue eyes, slim build, standing at 5'11" tall and Josh is 6'5" weighing around 265 lbs. Regardless of their appearance, they worked well together.

Michael put down the camera after taking a few more pictures of Roc. Detective Rayfield had teams watching Roc and Boggy 16 hours a day. They started this because Troy called in one day and asked to speak to Detective Rayfield, the head of the drug task force. Detective Rayfield knew Troy from the two times that he locked him up. He couldn't get anything on Troy so he couldn't believe his luck when he heard that his boss man of 13th street now wanted to talk.

At the meeting, Troy told them about the Get Money click and the men they shot but he didn't know who they were. He mentioned how he had gone to Roc for help but Roc just wanted his money so he wanted

Detective Rayfield to get Roc too. Now Troy was ready to make a buy from any one of them.

Detective Rayfield knew by watching the Get Money click that a war would come soon. They were raw setting up shop anywhere and someone would put a stop to it or die trying to for the money that they were taking. Detective Rayfield just didn't think they had the heart to try Roc.

Michael and Detective Rayfield still couldn't understand how they and the other team could lose Roc and Boggy for three hours and then receive an all car call to 7th St to find over ten bodies. Detective Rayfield knew that the war had started as the two cops talked while they followed Roc. "What do you think that was all about?" Detective Rayfield said to Michael. "I don't know but Lil man looks like he was not going for whatever it was," replied Michael. "Did they get any matches from the finger prints in the houses for Boggy or Roc's?" asked Detective Rayfield. "Not yet, but if it's a half of a print found....they are done. Look at this shit! Do you think they know we're following them?" Michael asked as he watched Roc speed up to about 85 mph making the light before it turned red. Suddenly there were three cars after Roc, coming on all sides with no way to go around.

Detective Rayfield thought he saw a smile on Roc's face in his rear view mirror.

Chapter 9

In a small row house that had seen better days sat the top dogs of the Get Money click, with Solo standing in the middle of the front room as the rest sat in chairs in a circle. Top Dollar was to the right as Solo started to talk, "By now you all know this is war. There is no doubt about that. So I need everybody on point at all times. When you pick up the block money, have five people instead of three, two cars instead of one. At the moment, all blocks shut down at 11 o'clock. And from now on you take your orders from Top Dollar. Just keep your eyes open because they know we are going to hit, but they don't know when. That is the only thing to our advantage so we're going to lay low for a minute until I get them where I want them. Are there any questions?"

"Did you hear anything about Dan and Veg?" asked Nay Nay. "No, not yet but I have the whole city on it," answered Solo. "Yo, you say all this like you know who did this shit," said D. Solo responded saying, "D, you still don't get it, do you? What would you do if someone was getting money in the middle of our two blocks?" D said, "I would kill…" Before D could finish his words, the thought hit him like a brick. Now he knew the pain that Solo was feeling because he too loved Roc like a brother.

"Are you sure, Solo?" Nodding his head up and down Solo to gesture he was. "So its war on Roc and Boggy, commented D. "It's the only way that he will respect us. But nobody is to touch Roc until I say so. I mean nobody! I don't care if you're ready to die and he has a gun to your head. Anyone who goes against this will answer to me," said Solo.

Top Dollar pulled Lil Mac to the side so that no one could hear him and said, "Young blood, this isn't right. Ya'll are family. We need to call Roc and talk this out so that we can try to get Veg and Dan back." Lil Mac abruptly replied, "Top Dollar, I can't believe this shit. I put you on top. You got a Benz, a B.M.W., big money, nice place and a team that will die for you. Now the question is…will you die for them?" "That goes without question, you dig. But you're my partner's seed just like Roc. So if there is any other way to handle this, then that is the way that we should go," answered Top Dollar.

"There is no other way. You know as well as I do that Veg and Dan are a done deal. They've been dead and there can only be one..." Lil Mac stopped talking as he started down the hall. He heard Top Dollar call out to him asking, "Only one what?" Lil Mac turned around and answered, "Boss."

A week later, ten of the Get Money click members were relaxing in the after-hours spot, throwing money like water at women. Top Dollar and D were arguing about who was going to buy out the bar this time. They sat in the back with three booths locked down. Bottles of Moet and Don P were everywhere just for them. D was chilling making a blunt while getting a lap dance from a big butt light skinned sin girl while Top Dollar was pouring Moet over her naked body. Solo sat in the booth just watching everything moving around them. He knew that when they were out, the player and the haters were on them. That is why Solo and Nay Nay never drank in public. That way, if anything popped off, they had a chance to see it coming.

The DJ started playing a song by Jay-Z as two girls came on the stage and started doing the damn thing to each other. Everybody started hollering and throwing money everywhere on stage. Top Dollar was at his best

73

when people were around, like he was onstage himself. He had on an old school London Fog hat, Prada cream and white suit with black gator shoes.

Top Dollar stood up in the chair next to the stage with a bottle in one hand and ten g's in the other. He was dropping money on the girls like it was raining. That's when somebody hit his leg softly. Top Dollar looked down to see the face of his old co-worker. He took one last look at the pretty girl on stage that was running her lips through the other girl's pussy hair.

As he put the bottle down, Top Dollar used his free hand to grab his gun that was in his suit's lower front pocket and said, "Yo, what up Troy…long time no see." Looking at all the money that Top Dollar had in his hand while he was putting his gun back in his pocket, Troy replied, "I see you ain't stopped getting money from the last time I seen you." "You know me. A real player can only be a sucker for so long, you dig?" said Top Dollar as he looked over Troy's shoulder at two men, one of which he'd never seen before. The other one was Fats. Top Dollar liked Fats because he kept it real. Troy could learn a lot from him.

"Top, I came to holla at you. I need some work for this new spot I got and I hear you're the connect," said Troy. "Slow up. First off...Troy who the fuck is this dude. I don't know nothing about no work and if I did, I don't talk in front of niggas that look like the feds," Top Dollar stated angrily. Troy attempted to introduce the man and was interrupted as Top Dollar said, "I don't care what his name is player...don't do that, you dig. If you want to holla at me, move by yourself or not at all."

Top Dollar never did respect Troy. He knew that Troy didn't have the heart for this game and he was hard headed. Now the sucker was trying to get put on. Top Dollar just walked away with Troy on his heels saying, "Top Dollar, that was my bad. I'm trying to get my hands on two of them things. For a good price, that's all. You know I'm not the po-po. I got hard years in the game."

"Yeah and so did Nikki Barns...but we do go back, so here goes my kick number. Holla at me in a couple of days and I'll let you know what's up," Top Dollar said. Troy took the number and walked the other way. When he was outside he started talking into the hidden microphone that looks like a button on his shirt.

As Top Dollar walked to the booths, Solo asked, "What did that sucker want?" "You know how these niggas are, you fuck them around now they want to get down. The vic's trying to get two cakes. I said I had to see first and told him to get back to me. I was thinking that we can give it to him at 26 a piece and make 12 off of him," replied Top Dollar. Solo looked at him and said, "Yeah we can…but do you think that he's playing fair?"

"That nigga's a sucker but I don't think he's on that side of the street," answered Top Dollar. "Just to be sure, you don't give him anything. Have someone we trust pass off because I don't like it. I'm going off of your call, and if he crosses us…" Solo was interrupted as Top Dollar finished his sentence for him saying, "He's a dead man."

Top Dollar pulled some money out and put it in a green thong of a dark skin pretty girl and pulled her towards him asking, "Pretty lady, is your sexy ass coming home with me?" She replied, "It depends on how much you're paying handsome." "I'm paying my name bitch…Top Dollar," he said as everyone started laughing. Top Dollar and the stripper walked off together.

A dice game was going on in the back room. When Solo walked in looking for Nay Nay, she had the dice in her hand talking shit. "Nigga double up on this eight. Drop another nickel down or let somebody with some money fade me. That's right nigga…you can't let a girl outshine you. Now watch me hit this six with a bowtie," she said.

The first dice stopped on two as the second one was still spinning. "You better stop them. That's six bitch's right there!" The dice stopped on six. "You niggas are hard headed, I just told you to stop them," said Nay Nay as she got the money from all around the table. The man that was paying her was hollering at the house man. "This game is fixed. There isn't a bitch on this planet that can win my money. Bet this right here," said the man as he dropped two g's. Nay Nay replied, "It's a bet but hold up so I can let my arm cool off, it's hot."

She passed the dice and started to talk to Solo, "What's the deal, Solo?" she asked. "I'm about to be out, I just wanted to make sure you're good," he answered. She wanted to say that she should come with him but didn't know what she would do if he were to say no. "Yeah, I'm cool. I'm going to get this money off these suckers, so I'll see you tomorrow," she said.

Solo jumped in his BMW 745il and was on his way to Roc's number two block so that he could put the last piece of his plan together. He stopped three blocks over so that no one could see the car he was driving. As he walked down Roc's block, people were everywhere trying to buy drugs before the spot closed. Solo stopped at an old blue and gray house in the middle of the block. He cut through the back yard and knocked on the side door two times, with one hard knock.

From the outside, this house looked like all the rest but the inside was lavished with top of the line rugs to the TV's built inside the walls. Only players in the city could get in, anyone else couldn't even try. After giving the special knock, the door opened and the man was ready to pat him down, until he saw that it was Lil Mac, his boss's brother.

As Lil Mac walked passed the man who'd seemed like a giant at 6'6" tall, he asked, "What are you doing down here again when you know them niggas want you for getting away with all that money the other day?" Lil Mac gave him a smile and said, "I got this...is Roc here?" The man replied, "Now you know Roc's not down here, if he was I wouldn't let you in. But if you need him he's down at the club." Lil Mac said, "Nah, I'm cool. It's on up in here."

"Yo, Lil Mac, I knew I would get your ass. That money was burning a hole in your pocket to come back to me. It's on now, it don't matter how you want to do it, let's just do it," said Mel 'Money Bags' Merricks. Mel was a big time player in the city who walked up and put his arm around Lil Mac's shoulder.

Lil Mac said, "What's up money bags, you still want to get it popping after what I did to you. I hit like ten numbers straight…that shit was crazy." Mel replied, "No doubt, they all are in the dice room now. I just came out for a bottle of Moet and got something sweeter…you!"

They both started laughing as they walked through the house. They went into the black jack room to show their respect to the players there, then into the poker room to do the same. Lil Mac did this each time he came there so that he would know everything about the place. This way, when it came time to put his plan in action, there would be no mistakes. Lil Mac made a mental note of all the bodyguards that Roc had on point and off the table. He knew the ones that were acting like they were in the game, but the whole time working for Roc.

Lil Mac and Mel stepped into the dice room to see players like Stevie Blue, Sammy 'Big Block' Gators, BA, Poppin tags shorty, fresh to def Billy, and about ten other top players from back in the day with old money. And the players of today were all standing around talking that fly shit. There was so much platinum and ice in the room you would have thought it was a jewelry store.

"There goes my player right there…Lil Mac, nigga you can just put your money in my pocket and stand there to watch me shoot," said Stevie Blue as he was shaking the dice at the head of the table. "What's the point?" asked Lil Mac as he stepped up next to him and smiled at this old head who had been getting money since the 70's. "Easy nine but I'm betting two dollars on nine and five." "Bet."

These players got real money so a thousand dollars was just like a dollar to them. "Where the bull Joe at, I need to get his money?" Lil Mac said to Mel. "He's down at the club; you know that thing open up next Friday. I'm going to be in the V.I.P. doing the damn thing with that shit on. You know how we do baby," answered Mel.

That was the fourth guard that Lil Mac asked about that wasn't there. After a week of coming there and three other spots, Lil Mac knew everything. By being Roc's brother, he could go to any place he wanted to and get the information he needed. Lil Mac lost a little bit of money and then left.

Chapter 10

Roc was setting up his upper office in his club called Soldi, which meant money in Italian. To get into the club, customers needed to have deep pockets. The night of the grand opening, Roc had everybody running around trying to get things together. This club was for the top ballers only, and charging fifty dollars just to get in the door. There wasn't another club around like it in the whole city.

At Soldi, you may get a live act on every floor in one night. Roc paid off a lot of people to make this happen. There were bottles of Champagne on ice at each table, food prepared by top chefs of the world. The room in the back of the third floor had some of the prettiest women of all shapes and sizes. For the right price, anything went, and showers were installed within the walls of each room. The V.I.P list started at two hundred and got higher depending on the floor that the guest was on. The list was sold out on opening night. Roc had people from many of the major cities in the country coming through.

However, Roc's mind wasn't really on his big day, instead it was focused on three people. The first was Lil Mac who he had not seen in almost three weeks. Roc still could not believe the way things went when he talked to Lil Mac that day. The three men he put on the store to look out for Solo said that they had not seen Solo or Lil Mac during the time that they'd been watching. The same girl opened the store every day and there was not a sign of another person except the two other women that worked there. Roc wanted Lil Mac to be there for this special night to hear his retiring speech.

The second person that was on his mind was Boggy. He didn't know how Boggy would take the news of his retiring and leaving him all the blocks. Roc knew that Boggy didn't need the money but he still left a million dollars in a safe deposit box. He planned to give Boggy the key after his speech. Roc just prayed that Boggy would understand why he'd made this decision.

Lastly, there was Solo, the man with no face but stayed in Roc's dreams. For the past few weeks he'd been waiting for Solo to make a move. When he didn't, Boggy said that they were probably scared off, but Roc knew better than that. He just hoped that Boggy was right on this.

The sound of his office phone ringing stopped Roc from daydreaming as he reached over to pick up on the fourth ring. "Hello, Soldi, how can I help you?" he said. A voice replied, "Man cut that bull shit out. You can save that for them suckers, I know you're a killer." It was Boggy on the other end of the phone, trying to disguise his voice as a white man. They both started to laugh.

Roc said, "Yo where you at man, you know that we open in a couple of hours and you still didn't tell me where you want your pictures hung up." Boggy replied, "You got the one when we were in Hawaii?" "Yeah man, there's about fifty pictures here" Roc answered as he remembered that day and all the good times that they had together in the life of the game. He looked at all the pictures he had enlarged and framed in gold for the walls of the club.

"You know its Friday and it's crazy out here. I got to lose this cop again. I don't know how you lose them so fast. I think they have about three teams on me. This one black girl working for them was following me and her ass is so fat that when she sat down it looked like she was still standing up. The bitch was giving me the eye too," Boggy said. "Get the fuck out of here…not the red bone?" Roc asked. "You've seen her too?" Boggy replied. "Yeah, she was on me for about a week until one day I walked up on her and told her that she needs to leave them alphabet niggas alone and get on my team. Boggy, I seen it in her eyes that she likes her man hard and dangerous so you can get it if your game is tight," Roc said laughing.

Boggy replied, "On the real Roc, that bitch is on me and I think I can bring her over if I go at her but only time will tell." "Speaking of time, why don't you get down here," insisted Roc. "As soon as all the money's in, I will be right there," said Boggy.

"You can get Haffee to do that. Just call the limousine service and get the H3 Hummer to pick you up. Be sure to put that shit on because you know how we shine on these cats," Roc told Boggy. "Haffee went to see his man out at the jail but when he gets back I'm going to pick him up, finish the pick up and then we're there. Is that all right with you, because some niggas still got to work?" Boggy said, finishing his sentence jokingly. "Nigga, fuck you," Roc answered as they started laughing again. They hung up the phone and

Boggy kept looking in his rear view mirror to see how far the dark blue car was behind him. There were two cops in it.

He rode for another five blocks until he saw a small one way alley. Boggy went on for another half a block then just stopped in the middle of the street. He then hit the gas hard as he made a U turn and went right passed the two cops while blowing his horn. Boggy shot down the alley out of the other side, just missing an on coming car. There were too many cars coming for the cops to get over and they knew that by the time they did, Boggy would be long gone.

Boggy and two men were in a gray mini van passing a blunt back and forth while they waited for Haffee to come out of his house. So they could go pick up the rest of the block money. Boggy knew he still didn't have to make these pick ups but he loved to stay on ground level so that he wouldn't lose the heart of the hustle.

"What's taking this nigga so long?" Boggy said aloud while looking at his caller I.D. seeing that Roc had called four times. On the second one, he had turned the ringer off and stopped answering his calls. Boggy hit the horn again just as Haffee finally opened the door.

"Here comes that nigga now," said Mike as he was getting in the back so that Haffee could jump in. "Haffee, ever since you touched back down you've been on some pretty boy shit, taking all day and not coming to the club no more....what's up with that?" Boggy asked while putting the car in drive and pulling off. Haffee replied, "It has nothing to do with no pretty boy shit. It's about taking your time in life. There is no need to rush life because the end will be here soon enough for all of us and believe me, when it gets here none of us will be ready. In this game we're in, we can die at anytime. So you need to take your time to live your life and please stay out of mine." "That's right Haffee, talk that Dr. King shit. These niggas don't understand, but I feel you nigga. You want to hit this blunt," said S.P. as everyone started laughing.

One hour later, the four of them were on the last block in the money house counting and wrapping up the money. When they were done, the two cars that were supposed to take the money away were already parked outside waiting. On the way down the steps to the car, S.P. and Boggy were talking and never saw the black van coming up the street or the black 4 Runner that was coming from the opposite direction.

Boggy was the first to see the man in the mask pointing his gun out of the 4 Runner but it was too late. He screamed, "Set up, get down" as a shot hit S.P. on the steps in front of him. S.P. was hit in the upper chest and in the shoulder, sending him spinning off the steps into the small yard. Boggy was blessed that the man was there to give him the time to whip out. He fired off five shots as he pulled Haffee to the ground but Mike wasn't so lucky, he'd taken so many shots from the Tech 9 that D was pumping, you would have thought he was doing the Harlem shake as the bullets pierced his body.

The people in the two cars never had a chance either. The five people in the van jumped out and hit the two people in the first car with over twenty shots within a matter of seconds. The second car's driver had started for the steps as Haffee and Boggy gave him cover. Haffee had a 45 in both hands returning fire with Boggy as they ran through yards trying to get away with their lives. The driver made it to the second yard before Nay Nay put four shots into him.

Boggy hit the first man that was running up the stairs three houses down from them. Haffee took out two more. Boggy knew they could not get boxed in or they were as good as dead. A person was moving along the side of the car like a cat, never took his eyes off of Boggy and Haffee. The person was now behind them. Haffee let off five rounds while covering Boggy as he hid behind a chair on the porch reloading his gun. He came out from behind the chair firing, the fire from his gun lit up the night as his gun downed two masked men, now one yard over. At the same time, Haffee took two shots himself. The first one hit him in his right forearm and the gun that he was holding flew into the air as he spun all the way around. Still firing from his left hand and pulling his trigger finger on his right like his gun was still there, the second shot hit him in the shoulder. This knocked him over the porch onto the ground between the two houses.

Boggy was firing on the man that shot Haffee when he saw something in the corner of his eye. Before he could turn all the way around, a shot hit him in the chest. Another shot hit him in his leg forcing him to the ground and making his gun drop. The shooter ran up on Boggy and put the gun to his head.

Chapter 11

Roc was dressed in an all white suit with a sky blue Armani handkerchief and matching tie. The blue belt and shoes that he was wearing were made of gator skin. His girl Gizelle had on the matching dress as they looked the part of King and Queen of the ballers. Gizelle was a thoroughbred and one of the finest women Roc had ever laid eyes on. She had been with him through it all.

Soldi was getting more packed by the moment. Roc went all out on his club and seeing all the people inside, and the lines extended outside down the block, made him feel that his hard work had paid off. Things didn't feel right without part of his team there. He called Boggy about ten times and still had not been able to reach him. Roc knew that he must have put his calls straight to voicemail like he always does, so he called Haffee. There was no answer on Haffee's phone either and then Roc decided to two-way Big Steve but again no one picked up. He pushed in one last number to no avail.

He had a bad feeling in his heart that something wasn't right.

Roc started asking everybody on his team if they'd seen Boggy and they all answered the same, saying no they hadn't seen him. Roc couldn't have a good time with this feeling he had. He went to get Buff over at the bar who was standing with a yellow suit jacket on and two pretty women on each side of him.

"Yo Buff, I need you to take a ride with me. I got to see what's up with Boggy and them niggas. They should have been here by now," Roc said. Buff knew just by the look on Roc's face that something was wrong. He was on his feet before Roc could finish talking. Buff threw three g's on the bar for the women and said, "Come on, we can take my car." Roc replied, "Ok, let me tell Gizelle to hold down the club while you bring the car around."

Roc went looking for his woman. It took a minute because of how crowded the club had gotten but he found her. She was giving out orders and making sure everything was on point. Roc walked up behind her, put his arms around her waist as he kissed her neck and said, "I'll be working for you next, pretty girl," She smiled as she turned around and said, "Roc, where have you been?

90

Blog of My Brother Yusuf T. Woods

You've got a million people asking for you." Roc replied, "Something came up and I have to step out, so I need you to keep doing what you're doing baby girl."

Gizelle gave Roc a passionate kiss and said, "Ok, but don't be long," as she watched him leave the club. She never asked Roc too many questions because they always respected their relationship and had the utmost faith in each other. Gizelle knew Roc better than he knew himself and was proud to be by his side on such a special night. She also realized that for Roc to have to leave so suddenly something wasn't right and she prayed that he made it back soon.

The masked man now stood with his 45 cocked and pointed at Boggy aiming the gun at his head as they locked eyes. He pulled the trigger twice while putting one bullet on each side of Boggy's face. Boggy thought that he was dead after the first shot but still never took his eyes off the two that were behind the mask. The masked man bent down next to Boggy as the police sirens became even more evident and said in a muffled deep voice, "In this game, it's kill or be killed but I can't kill you now. Not this time but maybe the next." Then he stood up, in the same voice saying "get the money, lets go," as he jumped in his 4 Runner with the van right behind it racing down the street.

Haffee heard the siren and knew he had to get out of there. When he made it to his feet, the pain in his shoulder and forearm shot through his body making him go back down to one knee. He tried his best to get back on his two feet to rush over to Boggy. Once there, he looked down and saw blood coming out of Boggy's chest.

"Boggy...Boggy, come on man you can't die on me," Haffee said. Hearing this, Boggy opened his eyes. "Man, we got to get out of here; can you move your legs?" asked Haffee as he helped Boggy up with his good arm. Boggy could barely walk but somehow made it to the van. Haffee opened the side door and laid Boggy across the back seat and pulled off. Haffee then ran every red light and stop sign there was while almost hitting three cars on his way to Broad Street.

He pulled up on the sidewalk in front of Temple University Hospital, with blood everywhere on him and went into the E.R. screaming, "I need a doctor now! Get me a damn doctor." Then he ran back outside to get Boggy out of the van. Moments later a doctor ran out the door asking him, "Where are you hit, sir?" Haffee

92

replied, "Don't worry about me, get my man." He pulled the van door open as more people from the E.R. came running out with a stretcher. Boggy was unconscious as they rolled him into the operating room.

Haffee stood at the window praying that his friend would be all right. After many attempts to get Haffee away from the window, a middle aged nurse put him in a wheel chair and pushed him into another operating room. Outside the hospital, D.E.A. agent Phil Giles was walking passed Boggy's van going back to his Ford Tempo after placing a 38 special under the back seat.

Chapter 12

"Top Dollar, make sure they set those cars on fire now. You know we can't go out like that baby boy," said Lil Mac as he put his arm around Top Dollar's shoulder. Top Dollar spoke to his man Ron about getting rid of the cars that were used tonight. After Top Dollar gave Ron his orders, he and Lil Mac jumped in Top Dollar's cream colored Benz with tinted windows. No extra stuff was needed because Top Dollar always said the rims and other extras told too much about the game. Top Dollar was from the old school and they didn't play like that. They just kept their cars clean.

They were doing 65 on the highway going to South Philly to Lil Mac's other house that only Top Dollar and Nay-Nay knew about. As Top Dollar made a left on Huntington Park, he said, "I don't know when you had time to put that plan together but it worked as smooth as a baby's ass. We were in and out but not before putting a couple of niggas down, you know how that goes. Man we stuck up everybody in the house. The blackjack and the poker room, they played it cool but the niggas in the dice game, I had to shoot like three of them hard headed cats. I even had to hit the old player Poppin Tops Shorty. You know me and him go way back like car seats. That shit hurt my heart to shoot him, you know?"

"Yeah I know Top, he used to run with you and my pop back in the day," replied Lil Mac. "So I'm like, why is this nigga putting me through this? He just made me shoot him and shit, now he got me feeling pain for shooting him and that's messed up. To feel pain for another nigga...that's some weak shit. Do I look like a weak cat to you?" asked Top Dollar. "No Top Dollar, there ain't nothing about you that's weak," said Lil Mac.

"You damn right, so I shot him again," Top Dollar stated as they both started laughing. He continued saying, "Yeah but other than a couple of players not wanting to give up their shit, your plan went great. They never knew what hit them. You picked the right time because they all were ready to go to Roc's club Soldi. Now we got deep pockets, you dig."

"Top Dollar, did you hear from Nay Nay yet? I talked to her after they hit the number house but she isn't answering her phone now," Lil Mac said. Top Dollar made another left turn then picked up the speed to pass 90 mph before he answered. "Yeah, she said everything went well but you know that girl, she likes killing people more than sex. She said she'll be at the spot tomorrow. You don't have to worry about her; she's all right, but what about you? I heard you had a top enemy soldier on the bus to hell and let him off?" It took Lil Mac some time to answer because at that moment he could see Boggy's eyes staring at him saying, "I know who you are."

"Lil Mac...Lil Mac," Top Dollar called his name bringing him back to reality. "Yeah Top, I had the Vic on the bus but the cops were coming and my team comes first. It was bad enough we had to leave Mike Raw and Rick behind. Boggy might not make it anyway." As the words came out of Lil Macs mouth, he hoped that they weren't true. But he knew that if they met again, someone was sure to die.

Top Dollar knew something wasn't right. They have been to the firing range together many times and Lil Mac was one of the best shooters he saw. He was ready to push deeper to find out what was really going on when his cell phone came to life. He answered on the second ring, "Talk to me." A voice answered saying, "It's me Troy. You told me to get back at you about them two things, what's good?" Top Dollar put his hand over the phone receiver and said, "Yo, this is Troy, what you want to do?" Lil Mac replied, "Like I said, it's up to you.

Top Dollar took his hand off the receiver and said, "Troy, where you at?" "I'm in G-town," Troy answered. "I will have someone down there to talk to you by Max's in two hours." "Bet." Top Dollar hung up with Troy and called KB who had been with the Get Money click since he came home from doing a five year bid. A cop had raided 13th street when he worked for Troy. When he was doing his time, Top Dollar always kept in touch by sending him money when he needed it. KB only had to do a two to five but stayed in so much stuff, he maxed out the whole five. When he came home, Top Dollar and the Get Money click had the block just like Top Dollar had said in his letters. Now he was a part of the Get Money click making more money in a week then he ever made. Top Dollar looked out for him when he touched down. He came home to a place of his own, instead of living with his mother. To him, Top Dollar was the only real father he had.

KB answered his phone sitting in his new drop top Saab, "Yo who's this?" He said as he turned down the car stereo. "Young man you trying to make some money or not," Top Dollar replied. "My bad, I didn't know it was you Top Dollar, I checked my caller I.D. and it didn't know the number you're calling from. What you got a new phone number?" KB asked. "Nah young cat, I got a new phone. I keep a chip burn out for a month or two then throw them away, you dig. So the feds can't tap your phone too easy."

"Yeah, I got to get me one of them. So what's up with this paper you're talking about?" KB knew when Top Dollar talked about money, it was time to listen because a come up was in play. "Troy needs two of them, for 26 each," top Dollar replied. KB was doing the math real quick as Top talked. That was 52 g's and all he had to give Top Dollar off two bricks he sold was 46 plus he was turning two of them into three by putting key of cut on two raw. The money just kept getting bigger. "He's going to be on Broad St. by Max's in a few hours. Just add four g's to what you already got for me and you can keep the rest. Can you hold that?" Top Dollar knew he just put a smile on the face of a man he loved like a son.

"I got that Top Dollar, all day," KB said. "Dig this-take somebody with you in case this clown is on some bull shit. This is the first time we're dealing with him after the situation, so be safe," Top Dollar advised. "I got this, if he get out of line…bye bye to the bad guy. One." KB put the car in drive and took off doing 70mph going straight through a red light on his way to get this money.

Troy was four blocks away from Max's in the back of a D.E.A. van with his man Fats. Fats looked on as the Agents and Detective Josh put the wire on Troy while Phil and Michael counted out the marked money needed for the buy. Fats couldn't believe they were doing this. He knew in his heart that this wasn't part of the game he grew to love. Even though Troy said after this they would get the lock back and be making that big money again, this still didn't sit right with him. Troy wouldn't listen.

Now it was Fats' turn to get the wire put on him. After they checked to make sure the sound was loud and clear they were telling them how to be a good CI. "Troy, make sure you say cocaine or crack when you're talking about the drugs," said Detective Phil. "Man fuck this, Troy let me holla at you outside," Fats asked as he opened the side door and got out with Troy following right behind him. "Fats, what you doing, man? You're going to mess up the deal," Troy said with the look of perplexity on his face. "Man, fuck that deal. I didn't make no deal, you did and this shit ain't part of the game. On the real I respect the Get Money click. They came and took the block like men because we were slipping. They didn't do this bitch shit, I don't respect this. Troy what are you going to tell your son when they're calling him a rat in school because his dad's a rat? This is going to get out. You're going to have to get on the stand and point these people out." He continued "let's just forget this cop shit and keep it gangster. We can get the block back like the G's we say we are because I can't fuck the game up like this. The game was good to us. It was all good when we were getting head in the six hundred from a girl we didn't even know. That came from the game. My five bedroom house, the trip to Japan, the five cars you got and your house in the suburbs...all came from the game. I guess the game was cool then, now a mother fucker comes at you and you turn straight bitch. Not me, I'm not going out like this." Fats opened his shirt and pulled the wire off his chest as Phil and Josh jumped out the van.

"Just the cops I need to see. Take this shit. Who says there's never a cop around when you need them? Troy, don't do this you'll be marked for life," Fats said." With anger Troy replied, "Man fuck what you're talking about. I'm trying to get back what's mine. I don't care what nobody says and if you're not with me…you're against me. Phil, lock this nigga up until I'm done the deal and then you can let this "G" go."

Phil gave the sign and two agents threw Fats up against the van and handcuffed him. When they were putting him in the dark gray undercover car, Fats screamed, "Troy, you fucking cop! I hope they kill your ass." The cop slammed the door on Fats. "Yeah, you're right, how much time do we have until these suckers get here, Phil?" asked Troy. "About 20 minutes so we need to set up now. The other team is already in place by Max's. Let's move," Phil replied.

KB pulled up on Broad St. looking around to make sure everything was all right. He saw Troy standing in front of the Eagle Bar smoking a blunt by himself. KB put the old Buick Century into park. He and Jay got out of the car. Jay put the book bag with the two keys in it over his left shoulder and they walked down the street. "Yo Jay watch this nigga, and keep your hands

101

on your gun cause if this cat even looks funny I'm popping him," KB said. Jay replied, "Man you already know I'm on it. I'm going to just stay in the cut until you give me the sign to bring the work and if shit ain't looking right, he gets it first."

"Here comes the kid KB now. He's with the Get Money click, watch him Phil, this kid is a cold killer," whispered Troy into his wire before KB walked up. "Smooth KB, What's up baby boy? Where is Top Dollar or are you the man?" Troy asked as sweat started to pour down his face as he tried to keep his cool. "Smooth? Come on man, I ain't in to all that. My name is KB, clown. What the fuck you sweating so hard for nigga?" Troy replied, "My bad KB. I got this cold that's why I'm sweating like this. You got the stuff because I got the money in my car and I'm not trying to be standing out here and then have the cops come by."

KB walked passed Troy into the Eagle bar without saying a word and took a seat by the window. Troy followed right behind him. The bar wasn't that packed, there were about 80 people enjoying themselves. KB had his eye on two white men in a dark gray Ford that was sitting across the street. "You see them two white men sitting in that car right there?" He asked Troy.

102

"Yeah I see them, why?" Troy asked, as he became more nervous and continued to sweat. If it wasn't for the air conditioning, it would have been more obvious and KB would have known that something was wrong.

"When the fuck did white boys start coming to Studio 37 in North Philly...at night?" KB commented. Detective Phil heard the conversation from his head phones while waiting in the back of the van and contacted the car that KB had his eyes on. Phil spoke into his walkie talkie telling them to get out of there right away. The car pulled off quickly as KB watched. Without hesitation, Troy tried to change the subject and quickly get things moving as he said, "What's up with the car? That doesn't have anything to do with us. I'm trying to get this and get out of here, you feel me?"

"All right, let's go," KB said as he stood up and put five dollars on the table. They walked out the door and he took another look around before telling Troy, "Go get the money and it better all be there!" Troy got the money from a cream colored 300C. He made sure that the cops were in place before walking back to KB. KB took the money then gave the sign to Jay who had been watching the block like a hawk.

Jay saw the two white boys drive off and come back around the block. They were now parked on the same side of the street he was on. He continued to watch them when KB gave the sign. Jay walked down the street as Troy and KB walked toward him and was about to hand over the bag when a car engine came to life behind him. Jay turned his head to see that the Ford with the white boys in it was speeding directly towards them. Seeing the bright yellow and blue D.E.A jackets, he dropped the bag, grabbed his two guns from his waist line and came up firing. He yelled, "5-0 KB." The driver took two shots in the face as Jay ran up on the passenger's side putting five into the next cop. The dark street was now full of lights.

Cop cars came from everywhere. Before KB could get to his gun, the shoot out was in full blast. A tear dropped from KB's eye seeing his man get hit with so many shots. "Get the fuck on the ground before I kill you too," an Officer said as a gun rested on the side of KB's head. They threw KB in one car and Troy into the other but the car that KB was in only had one stop and that was jail.

Chapter 13

Roc and Buff pulled up on the block to see cops all over. The yellow tape stopped the crowd from going down the block. As Roc and Buff jumped out the car, they could see some of the white chalk outline. Roc walked into the crowd and asked the young men standing to his right, "What happened here young buck?" One of them answered, "Man it was crazy as hell out here. Those niggas were shooting at everybody. They say it was the Get Money click. Two more people just got put in a body bag right before you walked up." Roc went into his pocket and handed the young man a hundred dollar bill and thanked him for the info. The guy replied, "Don't worry about it, Roc, anytime. You know me; I used to play ball with you and Mac on Sundays."

Roc looked at him realizing that he was a familiar face and said, "Oh yeah you're Gotti from Brooklyn's son, Cee's your name right?" "That's me," Cee answered. "So you know my man Boggy?" Roc asked as he pulled Cee to the side away from the crowd. "Yeah, I don't know if he was on the block when it happened but some cars did pull off right before the cops came and some of them looked hit. I'm not sure if it was him or not," Cee said. The words were like a brick wall falling on Roc's chest. Roc and Buff jumped back into the car and drove off. Buff sped up to 110mph as he raced through the city streets trying to make it to the closest hospital.

"If he was hit bad he would have went to Le Tempo because it's only a few blocks away." "Man if anything happened to Boggy I will kill the whole damn city to find out who did this if I have to. As they pulled up to the hospital, Roc saw the cops going through Boggy's van. Before Buff could stop the car all the way, Roc had already jumped out. Roc ran passed the cop into the E.R. and to the front desk. There was a middle aged woman sitting there and he asked, "Could you tell me if my brother Vincent Jackson is here?" The woman typed on her computer as she looked up the information and answered, "Yes we have Vincent Jackson here, he is in surgery right now."

Roc immediately started to walk passed the desk while at the same time asking the woman which operating room he was in. "Sir, you aren't allowed back here," she said trying to stop him. "Yes I understand but I need to find my brother," Roc replied. "Sir if you would please go back out front, I will find your brother's doctor and bring him to the front to speak with you," she tried to assure him. Roc attempted to walk passed the security guard but the guard put his hand on Roc's chest and said, "Please sir…" Roc interrupted and put the guards hand down off his chest before speaking to him. Roc leaned towards him and said, "If you ever put your hands on me again, I will kill you and everybody you know." He then turned and walked back out front and sat next to Buff in the waiting room.

"Is he okay? What did they say?" asked Buff. "Man I don't know any more than you do," said Roc. For about two hours, Roc paced back and forth until he was at the point where he was about to explode. Then a gray haired man with blue eyes came into the waiting room and asked, "Are you the family of Vincent Jackson?" "Yes, he's my brother…how is he doctor?" Roc asked. The doctor said, "Your brother suffered two gun shot wounds, one in the leg which went straight through. The other one was in the upper chest. His operation was successful but he will have to stay in the intensive care unit for a few days to make sure he heals properly."

"Doctor, can I see him real quick, I will only be a minute," Roc asked. "No one can see him right now. It's best to wait until he is out of the intensive care unit to minimize the risk of infection," the doctor explained. Again Roc said, "I understand that but if I could just see him for a minute I would be so grateful, I want to see that he's okay." Not realizing it, Roc had grabbed the doctor with his two hands and the security guard started to move closer and then stopped.

The doctor responded to Roc saying, "Sir, I realize that you are concerned and that this is a difficult time for you, but for your brother's safety I cannot allow anyone to go in at this time." Buff called Roc's name and said, "Come on I just got off the phone with Manny and Raja, they are going to meet us at the spot. We need to get to the bottom of this right now."

"You're right Buff. I can't help my man while I'm sitting here with my head down. Put around the clock security in here and get Woods on the phone. Its funny this was my last day in the game and now I'm going to make it the last day of life for a lot of people," Roc said.

Boggy was in room 203 on the second floor. When he woke up, he didn't know where he was or how he got there. As his eyes adjusted to the light he thought he was at a funeral as he looked around at all the flowers in the room. He tried to get up when two things stopped him; the pain in his chest and the handcuff on his right hand. Boggy sat up in bed halfway to push the button on the side of his bed. Five minutes later a black man about 5'11, brown hair wearing a white coat came into the room with a clipboard in his hands.

"I see you're awake, Vincent, I am Dr. Woods. Should I call you Boggy like everyone else does?" The doctor asked. "Call me Boggy, Dr. Woods. I can't have too many people knowing my government name." "I see," said the doctor. "What happened and what's up with these handcuffs?" Boggy asked. Dr. Woods walked over and shut the door before he started talking. "From what I heard, you were in a shoot out. Where...I don't know but what I do know Boggy is that you had a bullet in your upper chest that we removed it successfully. With the proper rest, you will be just fine. As for the handcuffs, there have been officers in here all week trying to talk to you but I didn't let them disturb you.

The medication we've been giving you could have you disoriented and saying just about anything."

Dr. Woods looked at Boggy closely and asked, "So you really don't remember anything?" Boggy closed his eyes and found himself right back in the middle of the gun fire a week ago. He reopened his eyes as the sweat ran down his face like rain and asked, "Doc, the man that brought me in here…is he okay?" Boggy questioned with a look of sincere concern on his face for his friend and soldier.

"Yes, Mr. Mayo is going to be just fine. He is down the hall in room 219 and he told me to tell you hello for him. Your friend Roc has been here every day until the D.E.A. started coming by four days ago. That is when he called me and asked me to call in some favors to get your case cleared. Now they are trying to talk to you, but if you are not feeling up to it, I will hold them off as long as I can. I must tell you though, you will have to talk to them sooner or later because they have the key to those handcuffs," Dr. Woods stated as he laughed and continued to tell Boggy, "Roc said your lawyer is now John Stewart. I hear he's the best on the East coast. These cops drop by everyday around 2:20 and if you want, I will be here with you. As soon as you don't feel like talking anymore, just say something hurts and I will get them right out of here."

"Doc, fuck those cops. I don't care what they know. I'm not telling them shit you can bring them in here now if you want. What's up with my man Roc and Haffee?" asked Boggy. "Haffee, as you know, is down the hall, he would have liked to come and see you but he too is handcuffed but other than that he's fine. Roc's like a whole different person now. You don't know this but he saved my life some years back and if that was not enough, he helped me to become the doctor you see standing here before you today. There isn't anything I wouldn't do for him."

Dr. Woods paused for a moment and then started to talk about Roc again, "That cold look in his eyes has returned, the look of death that I have not seen in years. At first I thought it was your situation that caused it, because everyday after work I've been going to see Roc since you've been here and he still hasn't had a hair cut. The man has over a thousand dress suits but keeps on the same dirty black hoody and sweat pants. All he keeps saying is to tell you two faces one tear, whatever that may mean. The fact is that there have been more bodies in here this week than in the last six months. I know you and Roc are like brothers and he needs you now to stop all this killing before he gets killed himself or ends up in jail.

Boggy knew Roc could handle himself better then anyone in the city. But Roc has been so laid back that it had been a year since he had to put in some real work. Now that it was on and he had the old Roc back, Boggy wanted to be right by his side. "Doc, when those gay ass cops get here show them right in. I need to get out of here to show Roc how it's done," Boggy said. "All right, now get your rest because you're going to need it," Dr. Woods replied walking to the door as he pulled out his cell phone to call Roc. "And Doc, it means when one person feels pain...so does the other," Boggy called out before Dr. Woods left the room.

At about ten minutes before 3pm, two plain clothes police officers were at the desk paging Dr. Woods over the intercom. Five minutes later they were at Boggy's bed side. "Vincent, my name is Detective Brian and this is my partner Will Lamar." Boggy didn't say anything, so Detective Brian continued, "Do I need to tell you your rights or can we cut through the bull shit Boggy...yes, I know all about you."

Boggy had been through this act many times so the poker face remained which was no surprise to the cops. "You don't have to read me anything because I haven't done anything wrong. Not only that my lawyer is John Stewart and you don't see him here, do you? So, yes cut the bull shit and tell me why I'm handcuffed to this bed," Boggy insisted.

"First, let's start from how you got shot and why," asked the detective. "I got shot in a dice game in South Philly when these two guys started shooting at each other, I just got hit in the cross fire," answered Boggy. "What did these two men look like?" I didn't get a look at their faces but I think it was two white guys if I'm not mistaken. No I think they were Chinese, or maybe it was two women." Boggy was trying not to laugh as he said this.

"Is that right, so you weren't in North Philly a few weeks ago?" The detective asked. "No sir, I haven't been in North Philly in years," Boggy replied. "You think this is a game, I have dead bodies all over 7th Street and I don't have time for games," Detective Brian said as he was getting very angry. Boggy, cracking a smile said, "Games, why would you say that?"

"You live in North Philly asshole, so you better start telling me the truth," demanded Detective Brian. "The truth is...fuck you!" Boggy's sarcasm made the detective furious as his face became red and he said to Boggy, "Okay smart ass I got two people upstairs saying they know who shot them. Yeah...they all weren't dead and so help me God if one of them points you out I'm going to put you under the jail."

Boggy's mind was going a mile a minute on a plan to make it out of there. Detective Brian picked up the phone on the desk and dialed upstairs. "Yes, this is Detective Brian. I'm ready to bring them down," he said as he talked on the phone. He hung up, looked at Boggy and asked, "What's wrong with your funny ass? You don't have any jokes now?" The detectives were laughing as the phone rang. Detective Brian picked it up on the first ring.

"What do you mean you can't find them? You better have them down here in two minutes or that will be your ass." Detective Brian slammed the phone down. Then he started walking back and forth in front of Boggy and asked him, "How did you do it? How did you even know they were here, Boggy? With a smile on his face, Boggy laid back and put his hand behind his head.

Detective Brian couldn't stand the look on Boggy's face. He got close to Boggy, nearly standing over him and said, "You think you've got it all figured out, don't you? You piece of shit!" Detective Brian threw a punch that hit Boggy in the side of the head and another that hit Boggy in the mouth. Dr. Woods pulled Detective Brian away from Boggy saying, "What do you think you're doing, detective? This man is in serious pain and you have the nerve to assault him? I want you to know that I am going to put this on the record with your boss." "I don't care if you put it on a record with God. I want that man out of that bed and on his way to jail in the next ten minutes!" Detective Brian demanded. "On what charge?" asked the doctor. "Gun possession," he replied.

Roc sat in the back of an Acura Jeep talking on his cell phone as Buff, Manny and Raja watched their target make a left turn onto the highway. Buff pushed the jeep passed 80mph so that the white M3 would not get out of sight. Now off the phone, Roc said, "Ease up Buff, his house is about five miles from here and we don't want to wake him up to the fact that today is his last."

In the last few weeks Roc had brought nothing but death to the city of Philly on his hunt to find out all he could about the Get Money click. The white M3

115

pulled into a blue and white three story house. The driver opened the four car garage with his remote as he drove in. Black jumped out wearing a three quarter length black mink coat, t-shirt, jeans and timb's. He opened the back door to his kitchen to let his pit-bull named, Blood, out.

Thinking that he had heard a sound, he grabbed his glock 10. He stepped out into his yard and moved slowly while his pit-bull pissed on the side of the house. Black walked to where he thought the sound had come from, finding nothing, but still not satisfied he called Blood to continue his search.

Manny moved smoothly behind the tree but never took his gun off the back of Black's head. It would be nothing for him to take Black out. "Roc, say the word and he's out of here," said Manny. "I need three more minutes," replied Roc. Black stopped walking and quickly dropped low and spun around to look from side to side before firing his gun. The shot just missed Manny's face as it took apart a piece of the large tree. The other shot hit nearly the same spot but a little more to the left was Manny's mouth.

Knowing that Black must've heard his voice, many backed away from the tree just as another shot hit

116

high. Manny started running into the open yard as Blood

began to run after him and Black opened fire.

Chapter 14

The sound of a gunshot woke Kim from her sleep. Thinking it was just a dream, she checked her clock that read 3:10am. When another shot echoed through the house Kim threw the blanket off of her body and ran down the hallway to the last door on the left. She opened the closet and grabbed her 38 mm off the top shelf.

Kim took the steps two at a time while taking her gun off safety. She hit the bottom of the steps and stopped like a pro, taking her time to make sure no one was in her living room. As she continued moving, she made her way to the kitchen and Roc stepped out of the darkness eating her potato chips. Kim spotted him and raised the gun to fire. Buff laid his gun on the back of her head and said, "Bitch drop it." Kim not knowing where he came from or how he got behind her dropped the gun.

Roc opened the door to the yard and called out, "Black, I got somebody that needs you for a minute."

Black turned to face his house and see his wife crying with a gun to her head. It seemed like his whole world came to an end at the sight of his young love in pain. Black would do anything for her to be okay even if it meant giving up his own life. "Okay, Okay....please don't hurt her," Black pleaded. A shot pierced through the darkness from Manny's gun, taking off the head of Black's dog, Blood. "Man what took ya'll so long. This nigga almost killed me." Manny said as he punched Black in the face.

Roc threw water on Black as he laid there unconscious. Coming back to reality his left eye was now closed and swollen. He also had four cracked ribs. As he looked around he saw his wife tied up beside him and realized that this wasn't just a bad dream. A voice asked him, "You know why we are here...don't you, Black?" Black really didn't but he also did not want to say anything to make the masked men mad. "The money is upstairs," he replied.

"Money," Roc said laughing. "Well, you've got part of it right, now let's see if you can get the rest." Roc slowly took off his mask and asked Black, "You know why I'm here now?" Black could not believe his eyes. It was the devil himself. He couldn't get the words to leave his mouth as hot piss ran down his leg. "Look at this fake ass nigga. I give you too much credit, soldier. You were just out back protecting yours by any means. When I saw that I said to myself, this young boy is going to go hard. Now you're in here wetting yourself in front of your wife. I know you don't want to die Black, do you?"

Black still couldn't speak so he shook his head. "I didn't think you did. So for you to keep your soul connected to your body, I need an understanding on the man named Solo," said Roc. When Roc finished, Buff put his Mac 10 to the other side of Kim's head so that if he shot her it would fly onto Black.

"Please don't hurt her, she has nothing to do with this," Black begged. Roc cut Black off mid sentence, "That's where you're wrong. She has everything to do with this. A part of me is in a cell that ya'll left for dead. So for that, every single one of you Get Money niggas owes me something. I'm talking down to the look- out men who just holler when the cops go by." Roc's face was about a half inch from Black as he talked through tightened teeth, "When I'm done, there will not be a person in the city that will sell ya'll bags to bag up with."

"Damn. I'm sorry I had nothing to do with that. I put that on my unborn. It was Top Dollar and them.

That's my boss," cried Black. Tears ran down his face as he talked to Roc. "I heard about Solo but I never really saw him. They work a closed circuit where one person can oversee twenty people, then reports to his boss. But those twenty people he oversees may oversee another twenty also."

"How do you get in touch with Top Dollar," Roc asked. Black answered, "I have his phone number but he changed it so many times, it may be on today and off tomorrow. I always text message him to meet on the dirty block where his old girlfriend lives. It's number 1116." Roc ordered Black to text Top Dollar now but Black said that he was in M.I.A. So Black wrote down every number that he could remember for Top Dollar and the other men who worked under him. Raja went upstairs and made Kim's bed before laying her body on top of it.

Roc walked out the side balcony door, the same way he came in. The sound of multiple shots in the background let him know that his clean up team had started their work. When they were done, there would not be a finger print in the whole house. Roc stepped out into darkness as a black tinted Lexus pulled in front of him and he got in sliding into the back seat.

"How did it go, kid?"

"The same as always old head."

"So he cried like a bitch?"

"You already know."

They both started laughing as the driver made a right to get back on the

Highway.

Roc pushed the 8 digit number to disable his home security alarm. As he entered his living room he could see a light on down the hall. Checking his watch it was 5:43am. Trying to think who could be up right now, he took his gun off safety and proceeded down the hall towards the cracked door.

The sight of Gizelle sitting at her desk, hard at work made a soft spot on his heart that had become so hard. Roc crept up behind her and kissed her gently on the neck. Gizelle closed her eyes from the feeling his touch. Roc nibbled on her ear, making Gizelle let out a soft moan, "Ooohh baby." As Roc spun the black leather chair around to face his only reason to love, his lips touched Gizelle's left eye then the right as he slowly unbuttoned her silk night dress. They passionately kissed while Roc worked his finger slowly and then fast in a perfect circular motion on the top of Gizelle's clit. The other hand was releasing her breasts. Roc sucked and bit

122

Gizelle's nipples hard and soft almost at the same time, sending waves through her body. She loved his smell on her. Roc kissed his way down her chest; touching every spot until he hit her love box. His tongue replaced his hand and he blew a light wind over her pussy lips before kissing them.

With every lick, Gizelle moved her neck side to side trying not to cum too easily from Roc's touch. She was still upset with him but all that went out the window when he gripped her ass cheeks to raise her to a higher position so that he could get deeper into her. Gizelle's juices glazed Rocs lips when her legs started to tremble as she came. Roc knew that he had her where he wanted her as he picked her up in his arms. He headed upstairs to the bedroom and laid her down on the pillows. "CD-2," he said and Aaron Hall's Interlude, *'You Keep Me Crying'* came on and filled the room through the surround sound system.

Roc slid into Gizelle, never letting her out of his arms. His wife's paradise fit super tight and Roc couldn't put all of his 9 ½ inch dick in without hurting her so he worked his way in more and more with every stroke. Gizelle's love box was so hot and wet, Roc long stroked her to feel every moment and part of her. She was mad at herself for letting her lust get the best of her. Now it was time for her to take over. As sweat ran off their bodies, Gizelle looked at Roc in the eyes and then in one smooth move, rolled Roc over onto his back without him coming out from inside her.

Gizelle started riding him long and slow. Roc watched as she moved her body up until the head of his dick was at the rim of her pussy lips and then made the whole 9 ½ inches disappear. Gizelle bent over and kissed Rocs chest, his ears and whispered, "Take it…it's yours" as she started to ride him faster. She put his hands on her ass and he spread it to get a better push. Gizelle could feel Roc was ready to bust and she jumped off his hard dick and licked up one side and down the other before placing it in her warm mouth. Her rhythm was fast and she took him deeper in her mouth each time.

Roc grabbed the back of her long hair to slow her down so that he could prolong the lovely feeling in a world that was so cold. But Gizelle would not be refused her victory as his cum touched the back of her throat. Gizelle got off the bed and walked into the shower. Roc followed, ready for round two when she slammed the door in his face.

Chapter 15

KB's feet touched the floor at the sound of his cell door opening. C.O. Myers walked in, handed him his morning newspaper and then left. "Get your dumb ass down and watch the door," KB said to his cellmate, Sun. Sun jumped off the top bunk and rushed to the cell door to look out for the officers. KB opened the newspaper to find his weekly stacks from Top Dollar. The four ounces of weed, two ounces of coke, some pills, a new knife and cell phone.

After bagging everything up and taking care of his celly, KB dipped down the tier with his wife beater showing and his orange county jumpsuit tied around his waist. KB knew he was the man of the jail. This was his first home. When he first got there, things weren't as sweet as they are now. The C.O. gave KB his cell, "You're in number 118, upper tier." KB grabbed the dirty blanket off the floor and walked out of his office. The inmates were watching his every move, some to see if they new him and others to see what they could get up off of him.

Everyone else was just eye hustling. "Yo that's the kid KB from them Get Money niggas," said Butter. "True life." "Yeah and I hear this nigga was eating heavy, pushing them things and everything." "Bet, go get baller and meet me upstairs," Big Moon said as he started walking to the steps.

KB opened the cell door and Sun was sitting on the top bunk reading Neglected Souls by Richard Jeanty. "Damn KB, what up?" Sun said as he jumped down to welcome his old friend. "It ain't nothing, Sun. Those crackers killed Jay," KB replied, shaking his head in disbelief. "I know, I seen it on the news man. That was messed up. You all right," Sun asked.

KB answered, "Yeah I'm cool, what's been up with you. The last time I saw you, you were getting that money out in West Philly." "Yeah it was sweet out there and then a lame got out of line, you know me I aired him out like nine times and the vic still didn't die. He dropped the dime, now I'm boxed in. But I will talk to you later, I'm going to go to the yard and get out of your way so you can get yourself together. The shower shoes are right over there, my locker's open. Take what you

126

need and them things is right here if something pops off."

"You're always on point," KB said. "You know it," replied Sun.

KB came out the shower with his sneakers on, a towel around his neck and shower shoes in his hand. All of sudden three men came at him, "Yo kid, are they the new Kobe's because they look about my size," Moon said. He stood about 6'2" and 310 lbs. "Damn how much that chain run you? I know it would look good around my neck," stated Baller. All three of them started to laugh. KB didn't say anything as he tried to walk passed but before he could make it, Moon grabbed him by the shoulder forcefully.

KB moving with the weight, turned around planting his right foot before throwing his left fist, slammed into Moon's rib cage. The right hand came right behind it connecting to Moons' eye. Moon dropped to the floor. Baller threw a fast hang maker at KB's head that he side stepped. KB sent a sharp upper cut down the pipe to Baller's chin that almost made him fall. Butter sucker punched KB with a two piece to the face that he didn't see until it was too late. KB rolled with the punches to lessen the impact.

Baller was back into the fight as they rolled on KB the best that they could. KB knew he could not go down on the floor or he was finished. Moon was getting off the floor. Seeing this, KB threw a five punch combo, giving himself enough room to run. Butter backed up from the punch he received. KB took off running down the hall and up the stairs.

"Run pussy, don't let me catch you out here again," hollered Butter. KB ran into his cell and pulled off the mirror to get Sun's two knives out of the wall and then ran right back out. "Ten minute move, ten minute move," came over the loud speaker letting the inmates know that they could move through out the jail. "Damn," KB said. He realized that the three men were no longer in the day room. KB walked around the tier looking into each cell. People stared at his closed eye and the big knife in his hand. He looked in the phone room and saw Moon on the last phone by the end. There was only one other person in the room who was using the phone by the door.

KB slid into the room and walked passed the first guy without saying anything. He went straight to work and pushed the knife hard and quick. The first hit went into Moon's lower back as he fell to his knees. "Oh my

128

God," Moon cried. "No nigga, don't cry now. Did you think I would let one of you fleas take something from me," KB said as he hit Moon 27 more times before he walked out into the crowd of people that were watching. As he passed the crowd he said, "Tell the other two, I'll be in my cell."

The news moved around the jail about how KB did Moon and was looking for the other two when they took protective custody. So after a few months of hitting the weights hard and thirteen more fights, KB's respect level was in the top ten. KB now sat on top of a table in the yard talking to a few of his fellow inmates. A man walked up to them and said, "KB, can I holler at you for a minute about some business." "Who's you main man?" KB asked him. "It's me, B.R. from C block. I'm trying to get some weight in trees for my man."

"So you're like a message boy or something. You're too old for that shit," KB replied as they all started laughing. "You could say that," B.R. answered. "On the real, I know who you are B.R. Lets take a lap around the track and get this money," said KB. They walked half way around the track talking about what the best deal was that B.R. could get for two ounces. B.R. stopped walking by a bench where one guy was playing solitary. "Just give me five hundred and you can get your man for two hundred because they go for seven," KB said. "That wouldn't be nice at all," the man playing cards interrupted. KB turned to face the card player.

"And who the fuck are you to be in my business," KB replied. "Boggy," he said. As the words left his mouth, B.R. stuck a knife deep in KB's neck. He was dead before B.R. pulled it out. "Yeah I'm a messenger boy for Boggy and Roc...get it B-R," said Chris as he and Boggy laughed and walked away. Haffee and Bo threw KB's body under the bench.

Chapter 16

After months of hard work, Get Money was a name to be feared through out the whole city. Even the top stick up boys knew when they came at Get Money to leave no witnesses because the price to pay was a hard death. The war with Roc wasn't giving them any ease, so for down time Top Dollar and Lil Mac stayed in M.I.A. a week after their meeting with their connect.

Lil Mac stood on the balcony of the presidential suite looking at the most beautiful skyline he had ever, seen when a nude sexy goddess handed him a cell phone. "Speak to me…what? Not KB, who did it Top?" Lil Mac asked through the phone. "We don't know anything as of now but Don is all over it," Top Dollar answered. "I know you loved him like a son Top, are you okay?" "I'm smooth, you dig. But when I catch the person who did this, I'm going to make Lil soldier proud," Top Dollar had a tear running slowly down his face as he spoke, "Things get deeper than that." Lil Mac stopped him and said, "Top, not on the phone. Pack up and meet me in the lobby in twenty minutes. You can fill me in on the way back."

As the G4 broke through the air, Top Dollar brought Lil Mac up to speed on everything that happened in the past week. "So he's dead too?" "Yes," Top Dollar answered. "What about Kim?" Lil Mac asked. "She's still alive but they said she is really messed up and hasn't talked to anyone since the whole thing happened." "So we don't know what really happened to Black either and they left a witness? This is unbelievable." Lil Mac pushed the button to recline his seat as he laid back and shut his eyes.

"What's unbelievable is how they got to his four under bosses," said Top Dollar. Lil Mac quickly sat up, "How could they do that when he didn't know them?" "I don't know but I'm sure we will find out. Until then I need you to stay low because we don't know what they really know or how they are getting their information. It could be one of us," said Top Dollar. "It's not one of us Top, or they or Roc would have been at me by now," Lil Mac replied. "Not too many people know you're Solo, give me some credit. I'll protect you well," Top Dollar assured Lil Mac. "That's why you get the big bucks," said Lil Mac.

When the flight landed, D and Nay Nay were on the runway to pick them up. Nay Nay told them about the trouble she had on her side of the city where she ended up having to kill people again. "Girl, I think you kill for a reason not to have sex," Top Dollar said. "I have sex. You're just mad I won't wrap these sexy legs around your old ass," Nay Nay replied. Everyone busted out laughing. "Girl if you were ten years older I would make sure you couldn't walk for a week." "If I was ten years older, your ass would be dead because when you could not get it up, I would kill you."

Top Dollar was laughing so hard a second tear ran down his face for that day. He was the first to get out D's 07 Tahoe as it pulled up near his peach Benz. Lil Mac rolled down the window, "Be easy old head. I'll holler at you in the a.m." "Okay and remember what I said. I need you to lay low until I get on these streets and see what's really good, you dig," said Top Dollar. "I got you. Stay low," Lil Mac rolled up the window knowing that laying low was not an option. He had his own plan to put this war to an end only one thing in mind, to win it all.

Top Dollar rolled down the highway doing 65 mph listening to the O'Jays. He had been back in the city for five hours, hitting every one of his spots trying to find out how much these people knew. At every spot it was the same story, they didn't know who was killing their team. Top Dollar made a right turn onto a small street slowing down to about 20 mph as he looked for a parking space. He was halfway down the block when a shot blew out his driver side window. "Oh shit," top Dollar ducked down as glass flew every where. Top Dollar stayed low with his feet on the gas as shots hit the Benz from different directions.

A shot hit the right front tire making Top Dollar lose control of the Benz. He scraped three cars as the sparks lit up and he hit an on coming car. Top Dollar opened his yes as he heard a voice call out, "Are you okay?" It was a dark skinned woman that stood at his window trying to open the car door. When the door opened a shot pierced threw the woman and she fell to the concrete. Top Looked to see blood coming from the woman's head and he ran for cover behind a parked car. With a 45 mm in his hand, Top returned fire not wanting to be a still target, he moved in and out of the parked cars.

Raja was hiding 50 feet away from Top Dollar standing by a telephone pole. He watched Top's every move. When Top Dollar moved down passed a few cars, Raja would slide to a closer pole. "Buff, shoot at the red car and when he pops his head up to return fire, I got him." Buff let off five rounds from his 9 mm blowing the window out of the red Honda Civic. Top Dollar rolled three cars down before firing back. Raja stepped out from behind the pole and didn't see Top Dollar sticking out underneath the car.

A shot hit Raja high in the shoulder and again in the center of the chest. Top Dollar slid from under the car and started running towards Raja to finish the job. Manny was closer to Raja than Buff. He came running out from the side of house 1116 gunning for the back of Top Dollar's head. Top Dollar felt the bullet fly passed his ear and changed directions. He ran across the street returning fire. Manny fired back as Top Dollar jumped over a fence.

Top Dollar fell face first into the yard when his foot didn't clear the fence. He quickly rolled over on his back and pointed his gun at the top of the fence, waiting on a face. When no one appeared he was back on his feet in seconds, running through the next yard. Manny's tech

135

9 came to life at the sight of Top Dollar. Top zig zagged back and forth when the bullets hit him in the back. The force from the bullets made Top Dollar flip and then hit the ground hard. He looked up at the stars, in pain as he lay on his back.

"Damn it….I can't go out like this," he said talking aloud to himself. His will to live got him back up on his feet. Manny was too far away to rush Top Dollar, so he took aim at Top's chest before he made it to his feet. The tech split widely as it tore pieces of the wooden fence apart. Top Dollar ran for cover. The sound of police sirens grew louder in the background. Manny knew it wouldn't be long before they made it to him. He watched Top Dollar run up the steps to a house and kick the door open.

Buff put Raja in the car and spoke into his ear piece, "Manny…it just came over the police scanner that the closest cop is two blocks away, let's go." "I need more time," said Manny. His feet touch the steps of the house Top Dollar just went into. He reloaded the sixty-four shot tech 9. "You don't have more time, get back here," Buff replied.

"What about the O.P.?"

"The O.P. lives to see another day."

136

"Roc's not going to like this"

"That's why you're going to tell him."

Top Dollar ran straight through the front door and out the back into the backyard making sure no one was following him. He ran down the alley and pushed number seven on his speed dial. The person answered on the first ring and he said, "Solo, the bitches tried to hit me."

Chapter 17

Sunday was a beautiful 85-degree day. The sun rested high in the sky without a cloud in sight. Roc sat in the back of this old head, Mr. Holmes' pearl white Benz 600 reading the morning newspaper. Mr. Holmes pushed the Benz and drove down an old country road going 70 mph, watching the trees fly by when he asked Roc, "Son, don't you think it's time to hang your shoes from the phone lines?"

"Not just yet old head...but soon," Roc answered. "Soon? You say that like you can pause this game you're in. Know that this game is death, don't ever forget it. Do you remember the first thing," Mr. Holmes said. Roc replied, "Come on old head, not now." "What...I asked you if you remember," Mr. Holmes responded angrily. Roc answered him, "Yes. A feared enemy must be crushed completely." Mr. Holmes told Roc, "Now you have become the fear and as soon as you let your guard down there will be another click coming after you. After that there'll be another and another and so on."

"That's understandable, old head. Everybody wants to eat but it's my name that is on the plate. When it's my time to go I will sub my damn self out of the game...not foul out." "Roc, have you completely lost your mind? You sound like you did when I gave you your first key ten years ago. I know you have become way smarter than that. I made you smarter than that and I raised you better. The only thing this game is for is to provide an opening when you're lying on your stomach and your back is touching the ground. It comes at a high price, so if you're blessed enough not to be in a box, your family is straight and you possess wealth, why won't you let me bring you up to the next level and get this corporate money? Put that newspaper down and look at me when I'm talking to you!"

Roc put the paper on the seat beside him and smiled at his old head knowing that he was only trying to help. "Believe me, I feel everything you're saying and I thank you for every thing that you have done for me. I know you took time out for me because you saw something in me. I really don't want to let you down but as I walked through the shadow of death, I became the shadow of death. Because of that, I lost a lot. I lost Lil Mac; he has not even returned my phone calls. I lost Boggy and I feel like I'm losing Gizelle too."

Roc looked out the window for a moment in deep thought before he continued talking to Mr. Holmes. "You taught me that a feared enemy must be crushed completely because if you leave him with one soldier, he'll be back to fight harder another day. It's for this reason Solo must die. Then and only then, can I move forward in life. I've got to finish my breakfast."

Mr. Holmes said, "Okay Roc, let me ask you this question. Do you know how many people I put on that had maxed the game out? Believe me it wasn't many but the ones that did, the game will remember for a lifetime like ET, Deek, Turtle, Aaron, and Maxxie. You saw the outcome of all their situations." Mr. Holmes stopped at a black gate. Roc rolled the tinted window down so the white man in a blue suit could see his face from his office. The man pushed in a few digits on his keyboard and the gates opened. The Benz moved slowly through the cemetery, and then stopped along side the clear road.

"No disrespect to any of them but I'm not them," Roc said to Mr. Holmes. "I know but you have maxed out the game as well, so what's next?" Mr. Holmes

140

asked. Roc opened the car door and said; "Only time will tell." He got out while Mr. Holmes remained in the car. Roc walked through the grave yard until he stopped at a black and white marble sculpture of an angel head stone. He bent down and pushed the leaves away before he laid his flowers at the angel's feet.

Roc began talking, "What's up Dad, how are things in heaven? I know the big man up there is treating you right. Down here Mom is still as beautiful as when you left her. As for me, I'm still not letting anybody stop me from feeding my family. If I got it, I'm definitely supposed to have it. I got Mommy that house she always wanted. I just wish you were here with her. Dad, I need you to ask God to turn his head the other way for a minute. I tried to tell your main man, Mr. Holmes, that I have to finish what I started. That would mean a lot of people are about to come up and see you or down to see the devil. It really doesn't matter which direction they go, as long as it's not here."

The sound of a car approaching made Roc turn and see a dark green car slowly moving down the road. Not recognizing the car, Roc turned his attention back to his father. "Me and Gizelle are still hanging in there and trying to make it work. Dad she's a good girl. You would

141

love her. She's beautiful, plus it doesn't hurt that she has a big ass, just like you like them with that apple shape. I know you're laughing right now. I remember you always telling me to be my brother's keeper too. Unfortunately me and Lil Mac aren't seeing eye to eye right now. I know we're family and blood is everything…things just aren't the same."

"What are you telling him about now, when did you start that?" A voice said as Roc jumped up. "How long have you been there," Roc asked seeing that it was his brother. Lil Mac replied, "I've been here long enough to hear you telling daddy on me." Roc said, "I must be slipping Lil Mac." "No, you're not slipping. I'm just moving better. "Man come around here and show me some love, I haven't seen you in a month. Damn you're getting big."

The two brothers embraced and Lil Mac closed his eyes on contact, hating the feeling of what he had to do to Roc. "How did you know I was here?" Roc asked. "Come on, its Sunday. It hasn't been that long after all the games I beat you in. How could I forget that we come here after every one? Not only that, I wanted to talk to Daddy anyway," Lil Mac said, lying about his reasons for coming there.

"Whose car you got? I see it's clean," Roc asked. "That ain't nothing, I had to charge my look up to lose the yes so I exchanged the Acura for that and you know green is my favorite color," Lil Mac told him. Roc and his brother talked for hours and Lil Mac promised to go out to dinner with Roc the next day. Roc loved the fact that Lil Mac was back in his life and Lil Mac loved how smoothly his plan went into motion.

Chapter 18

It was Friday, the 1st of the month in West Chester, Pa. The Sidetrack apartment complex was in full swing, doing its numbers like always. Money was coming from all different directions as hustlers ran in and out of the buildings to re-up. Troy returned from beside the C building selling another ounce with his body guard Eric on his left. "I told you it was sweet out here," Troy said. "Yeah it's like 92 out this bitch, so when you going to let me kill some of these sweet cats and get some of that money off of them?" Eric asked. Eric was a dumb stick up kid with a quick temper. He used to put in some small work for Troy when he had 13th Street. Eric would shoot anybody for the right price.

The word got out fast about Troy being five-o so there wasn't too many people Troy could turn to. He had to move his family quickly and he brought Eric with him. They were moving from town to town for months until Troy ran into his ex-girlfriend Liz who lived in apartment building C. Troy came through one late night for a booty call. Seeing all the traffic going back and forth, he put in some overtime on Liz's ass to pick her brain for all the information on the layout. Liz being the hood rat she was, knew everything there was to know, and told it. Troy got Eric from Downingtown, Pa where they'd been staying. Eric was wanted there for 4 bodies already.

Now Troy paid and sexed Liz to keep his drugs in her apartment. The money came slow at first but after a little time being out there, Troy was now eating hand over fist and he and Eric stopped short of a cee low game. "E, I need you to chill out on this killing shit. I got these suckers in pocket and in a minute I...I mean, we will have this whole complex on lock and then Oak place. You want to own all of this, don't you?" "Yeah, but look at all that money on the ground," Eric said pointing at the cee low game a couple feet away. "I didn't get any money, I can kill them and take that money right there."

"Man, you don't need no money, I got the money...here take this eight ball," Troy said. Eric took the crack and started to put some into his Newport. Troy stepped up to the dice game as Danny was about to shoot. Danny was a big money hustler out of the building

A. "What's in the bank, Danny?" Troy asked. "Six g's but for you I'm taking all bets because you act like you're like that when you're not," Danny replied. The crowd busted out in laughter. Danny wanted the same thing that Troy was after, the complex. He had been home for over two years.

Danny was from West Chester, PA and he had over half the complex on lock, so there was no way he was going to let an out of towner get his money. Troy was a hustler by heart before anything so he had taken more sales from Danny every day and his coke was better. "Come on Danny, you really don't want to do this, man. I got old money don't let this shit you see fool you. There are too many girls out here to let you play me," Troy said.

"Man, name the bet or shut up. I'm sick of you niggas coming out here faking it," Danny replied. Troy was a lot of things but broke was not one of them. The crowd now was in a circle waiting to see which player was the realest. Some cheered for Troy but many called out for Danny. All and all, it was just another Friday.

Troy pulled Eric to the side to talk to him and then Eric ran off. "Bet all of that trash right there and hold six." "Bet," Danny shook the dice then let them fly.

"Four five six on him," Danny shot the dice three times before catching his number four. Troy grabbed the dice and said, "Bet another two g's. I'm five or better." A person from the crowd shouted out, "Danny, don't let this out of town nigga try to play you out here." "I got this cat all day, like I said the first time…I'm taking all bets," Danny said. "I know player. You got it all day," Troy added as he smiled and let the dice go. On his second shot the dice stopped on two, two, and five. "There she goes," Troy hollered out as Danny dropped another two g's on top of the six.

Danny asked for the next bet. Troy said, "Bet this eight on the ground. Danny's next shot made the dice go all over the place before stopping on four, five, and four. With the dice in his hand, Troy said, "Bet four g's." "I got five or better." "Bet." Another person from the crowd yelled, "That nigga Troy is the real deal." The statement made Troy step his game up. His next was also a five. Danny bent down to grab the money when Troy stopped him and said, "Man, what are you doing? That ain't your money." Eric stepped on the side walk and handed Troy a mid-size brown paper bag.

"Why? It's all pushes paid."

"Hold up, first off you didn't state any rules on your bank. That's not in one on one."

"All right we'll shoot it over. What's the bet, the same thing?"

"No, you just tried to get over on me on some flea ass shit. I hit the five so owe two g's that makes it ten. Bet this on top of the ten."

Troy went inside the brown paper bag and dropped two more knots on the ground. "Bet that twenty g's." Danny could feel every person in the crowd looking at him. He felt that he might be out of his league for the first time as he called, "Bet". Danny put the dice on four, five, and six then locked them inside his fist tightly. He shook his fist wildly never letting the dice move in it. Slowly he let them go almost as if he'd set them down on the ground.

The first one stopped on one, next number was two, and then three. Danny almost fell on his face when he saw the last dice stop on three. Being the player he was Danny dropped the money he had on him, and then ran across the street to his apartment to get more. He came right back. Troy had Eric pick up the money and then said to Danny, "You ain't had enough of these golden arms, nigga?" Troy replied, "I'm here, what's good?"

Danny pulled out two nice size knots from his Polo jacket. Seeing the money, Troy saw blood and went in for the kill. "Now let's see who's really faking it, bet the bag." Troy dropped the bag on the ground at Danny's feet. "How much is in it," Danny asked. "I don't know. Something small, it's probably about 40 or 50 but that ain't nothing to you player, you take all bets," said Troy. Then he opened the bag so that Danny could see the money.

"I don't have that much on me," Danny told Troy. "All you have to say is it's a bet and then shoot the dice. You're good for it, right Eric?" Troy said as he looked at Eric who was standing nearby with his hand on his gun as he shook his head. Troy loved these moments to show he was a big shot. "No bet," Danny said. The crowd went crazy when Troy responded saying, "I'm sick of you niggas out here faking it. Danny if you want some real money get at me, don't nobody want to try to get at this money." Troy knew that the day had come and he was the next King in all their eyes.

"I'll take some of that money," said a pretty girl wearing baggy jeans, t-shirt, and Timbs as she stepped into the center of the crowd. She had two guys by her side. "Damn sexy, you're telling me you've got 40 g's on you?" Troy asked. "No but I got enough," she answered while pulling out a knot of money from a deep pocket in her jeans. The crowd was going wild again as they cheered the girl on because she had the heart to step up.

"I like to shoot two dice," she said. Troy replied, "I do it all baby girl." "Pee wee ace high six better." "Nah, you go on and shoot them." She let the dice go and the first one was a three, the second stopped on one. "Little Joe, I killed that nigga last week and was…" "Seven bitches," She finished Troy's sentence. "How you know I was going to say that sexy?" Troy asked her. "Because she heard it before," said a man standing next to her on the right.

Troy remembered the voice but couldn't put a face to it. Then it hit why, because there never was a face…just a mask. Troy turned to Eric and gave him the sign to shoot. Troy couldn't believe his eyes, the sight of Top Dollar blowing the back of Eric's head off. Everyone ran in different directions to get away from the gun fire. D was the first one to point a gun at Troy from beside Nay Nay.

"Don't move!" "Top Dollar, I didn't do it, I swear I'm on the run right now. That's why I'm out here," Troy tried to explain. Top Dollar pointed his gun at Troy, and then Lil Mac and Nay Nay pointed their guns. Top Dollar said to Troy, "Tell KB I set you, but before you go…Fats said hi." They all fired on Troy until there wasn't a bullet left in any of their guns.

Chapter 19

Haffee sat at his desk in his cell reading the book *'Why the Word Salfai and Who Are the Salaif'* compiled by Abu Abdullah Muhammed Islam Alyahimi Alumr Abdullah. He was getting his mind ready for Jum'ah when the cell door opened. Boggy looked up from his bed as the correction officer told Haffee, "Mayo, you have a legal visit. Get ready." "Boggy, did you talk to John or Sam and did they say they were coming to see us?" Haffee asked. "No, they didn't say anything and neither did Roc but you know we start trial next week. They probably just want to make sure they have everything ready," Boggy answered.

"I better get ready because they are going to call me next and you know that girl I sexed last week stopped talking to, she's funny. She works at the desk down there but I'm trying to hit tonight. So let them know I'm coming down next," said Haffee.

Five minutes later, Haffee walked into the visiting room. He looked around for his lawyer Sam Clinton, but when he didn't see him, he asked the officer sitting at the front desk to tell him who he was there to see. The corrections officer looked at Haffee's name tag and checked the clipboard. "Mr. Mayo go wait in that room right there and they will be with you in a minute," the officer said.

Haffee sat at the table in a hard wooden chair when Detective Rayfield and Michael walked in and said, "How are you doing, Mr. Mayo?" Haffee jumped out of his chair and headed for the door as Detective Rayfield blocked his path. "Let me out of here pig! I'm not with this," Haffee told the Detective. "Mr. Mayo please have a seat, we just want to talk to you. You don't have to say a word if you don't want to," he replied.

"Yeah, you're right," said Haffee as he knocked hard on the glass window to get the attention of the correctional officer so that they could open the door. "Yo, get me out of here and take me back to my cell," he screamed. The correctional officer looked at them and asked, "Are you all done in here?" Detective Rayfield replied, "Not at all." "Okay, take your time and Mr. Mayo asked Boggy if he's still not speaking," the correctional officer said as she smiled and walked back to her desk.

"See it's not that easy to get rid of us," said Detective Rayfield. "Man, say what you have to say so I can get away from your pork ass," Haffee replied. "I see…so I guess I should get straight to the point Mr. Mayo. I don't want you. I want Roc and Boggy, so if you give them to me, I will let you go." Detective Michael said, "I think that deal is too nice for you Mr. Mayo. You should do at least 20 years, but it's not my call." Haffee responded by saying, "I would love to see you give me 20 years for a gun charge that I'm going to beat on Monday." Haffee laughed in their faces.

Detective Rayfield said, "It's funny? It won't be funny when the 848 indictment comes down and the feds give you life. But I don't want that to happen to you Mr. Mayo. I want to help you. Don't think for one minute that we don't know about Kevin, also known as KB. It's only a matter of time before someone tries to help themselves and we get you for that. I know you're not the killer. That's Roc and Boggy, so help me help you."

Haffee didn't say anything. Detective Michael said, "See Detective Rayfield, I told you this good for nothing piece of crap wouldn't know a good deal if it bit him in the ass." Haffee jumped up and threw a punch at Detective Michael hitting him right in the face. Detective Rayfield grabbed Haffee from behind as his partner got himself together. "You dirty bastard," Detective Michael said and then hit Haffee with five punches to his rib cage and ending with an upper cut to the face.

The correctional officer saw what was going on and hit the deuces on her radio to call for back up. More correctional officers came as Detective Rayfield let Haffee go and then punched him in the face. The punch made Haffee fall back against the wall. Detective Michael was back on Haffee throwing blows when the officers rushed in the room pulling the Detective off Haffee. Blood was running down Haffee's mouth as he spit in Detective Michael's face.

"You're finished! You're finished Haffee...you're a piece of shit and you'll never see your kid again," screamed Detective Michael. Haffee turned back to face them after being handcuffed by the correctional officer's and said, "You say that like Allah doesn't have a say in all of this." The officers walked Haffee back down the hall. Sun watched the whole thing as he sat in the visiting room with his wife. Boggy laid on his bunk smoking a blunt while talking on his cell phone. He was thinking about what he was going to do to the sexy dark skinned woman named Deja who was on the other end of the phone.

"Girl, I don't even know why you're playing like that. I don't jerk off. If it's not the real thing, my man don't stand up," Boggy said to her on the phone. "It will stand up for this thing here. All you have to do is put it to the phone and it can smell the love of my lips from there. You know you can't get enough of my wet walls," she replied. "Is that so? You weren't saying that when I had you chasing down my car on Broad street. Stop Boggy Stop...I can still hear you now," Boggy said as he started to laugh.

Haffee walked into the cell and Boggy looked over to see him. "Oh shit what happened to you...who did this?" Boggy hung up the phone and pulled out Dane and Bruster, his two knives that he always kept in his waistline. Haffee answered him, "Rayfield and Michael," and told Boggy everything that happened. Haffee's eye was closed and his lip was swollen. Boggy couldn't stop laughing. "What's so damn funny Boggy," Haffee asked. "That fucking Rayfield sucker punched me too. He be trying to get his man for real. It's too bad I got to kill him. I was just starting to like him," said Boggy and then he picked up the phone and dialed ten digits.

Roc answered the phone, "Soldi, Odell speaking. How may I help you?" "I guess you're a real business man. Roc you're killing me….what did I tell you about that bull shit," Boggy said. A smile came to Roc's face instantly hearing from his best friend. "What's up dawg? You know you're coming home next week and that's on me. I'm sorry I couldn't get you bail but them crackers aren't playing fair so I sent in some help, you know how I do it," said Roc. "Yeah…you could have sent anybody and you sent Chris and Bo, they stay in something. If we don't get out next week, come and get them two because they are going to end up catching a new case," replied Boggy. Roc laughed because he knew Boggy was telling the truth.

"How's Haffee doing?" asked Roc. "He's right here," replied Boggy. "Tell him I took care of his parole officer for the rest of his life. He doesn't have to worry about another violation," said Roc. "That's why I called. Detective Rayfield and Michael came out here and tried to flip him," said Boggy. "Haffee ain't going for that, that's not about anything," said Roc. "I know but they crossed the line when he didn't talk. They rolled on him.

157

If you could see his face…they fucked him up," Boggy replied. "Enough said, done deal," Roc said cocksure. "And Roc, leave Rayfield for me," Boggy requested. "One," said Roc. And "One," replied Boggy.

Roc put the phone back on its bridge and laid back in his big black leather office chair. "What's up with Boggy…is he all right?" Lil Mac asked Roc. "Yeah Mac, you know Boggy's a warrior. Whatever it may be, he will take it. You ready to go?" said Roc. "We can do that, I just got to use the bathroom real quick," replied Lil Mac and he walked down the stairs into the first floor bathroom. Once inside he locked the door behind him and pulled out his cell phone. "Top Dollar…in the nest in 20 minutes," Lil Mac said on phone.

Roc pulled away from the curb in his new Hummer sitting on 28's. The base could be heard a block and a half away as he and Lil Mc moved through the street. "When did you get this Roc?" Lil Mac asked. "Why…you like it?" replied Roc. "Yeah, this thing is hitting," said Lil Mac. "I really didn't want it but old head said if you hit and miss, you get something like this. Do you know what college you wanted to attend yet or are you still playing around?" Roc asked. "Believe me

Roc, I'm thinking about Oxford or Temple but it looks like my future is getting better everyday."

Roc and Lil Mac had been hanging with each other just about everyday after they had dinner together two months ago. Lil Mac was now working at the club helping Gizelle keep things together. They were even playing ball again on Sundays.

Chapter 20

Roc was sitting at a red light looking in his rearview mirror checking out the two beautiful ladies in a gold Lexus that were kissing each other when he recognized the same black Tahoe he saw four blocks over also. Roc didn't say anything to Lil Mac because he didn't want to scare him. For a moment Roc thought that he was just being paranoid but he was going to play it safe.

As he rode through the green light, he made a right instead of a left like he was supposed to. "Roc, you're going the wrong way, "said Lil Mac. "I got it…we'll be at the gym in a minute. I just have to make a quick stop, "replied Roc. He decided to speed up and pushed his Hummer passed 65mph. The Tahoe fell four cars back but Roc could still see it so he made another quick right and then parked in the first parking space available. Roc pulled his 45 automatic out from the center of his back and brought it around on his left side, hiding it from Lil Mac's sight.

Roc hid the gun between the door and his body as he watched every car that passed closely. A few minutes had passed before Roc pulled back into the traffic. Lil Mac looked as if he was playing with his phone but was actually texting Nay Nay and telling her to back off. "Are you okay? You don't look too good," Roc asked. "I'm fine. I'm just trying to work out that's all," Lil Mac said while he wiped away the sweat from his forehead. Roc pulled into the top level of the Y.M.C.A parking lot

"There they go right there," Top Dollar said as he pointed at the Hummer that Roc and Lil Mac were in. D pulled his mask over his face and Top Dollar made sure his 9mm and 45 were fully loaded. D tightly gripped his gray tech 9 as he eased out of the car. He looked Top Dollar in the eyes before closing the door and said, "This is for Veg, Dan, and Catty." Then he ducked down low as he walked slowly through the parked cars. Top Dollar told Nay Nay, "Be ready on three." Nay Nay's team of six got themselves on point in the back of the Tahoe. Nay Nay put the truck in drive moving at 10mph until she was three cars away from the Hummer. D and two other men stood on Roc's side of the Hummer, one car over.

Roc was on the phone talking to Gizelle about their plans for dinner at Justin's in New York. Lil Mac saw the masked men when they came up from beside the car. Lil Mac ejected the c.d. out of the disc player and leaned into the back seat to appear as if he was looking for a new c.d. Roc didn't see D until he had a tech 9 at his window. D pulled the trigger. Lil Mac braced himself for the shot as the shot ricocheted off the bullet proof window.

"You motherfuckers," Roc yelled and put his Hummer in reverse. Seeing the white lights come on, Nay Nay pushed down hard on the gas trying to block the Hummer in. the six men jumped out of the truck and started firing on the Hummer to no avail. "Lil Mac, stay down," Roc said and then he stepped on the gas as he slammed into the side of the Tahoe. The row bar on the Hummer made the Tahoe slide back three feet. Then several bullets hit the front windshield.

Four of the men tried to save Nay Nay from being flipped over onto her side. Roc slammed into her for the third time now, each time he made contact with the Tahoe it went higher into the air. Roc put his feet all the way down on the gas and then slammed the Hummer into drive. The Hummer jumped forward running over two of

162

the shooters that didn't make it out of the way in time. Roc turned the steering wheel hard to the right, setting the Hummer in a different direction with the driver side door facing the shooter.

  Roc ducked his head low and cracked his window a little, giving himself enough space to stick his Mack 10 through it. Then he started firing and when Lil Mac saw his men dropping, he tried to grab his own gun. Throughout all the commotion Lil Mac had forgotten that he didn't bring his gun with him when he was with Roc. Top Dollar was watching the whole ordeal, waiting on the right moment to attack, when Roc pulled the Hummer about twenty yards in front of him. Top Dollar was on the blind side when Roc had cracked his window and now only saw one way to end this. Top Dollar knew he had to put a bullet right over the spot where Roc's gun rested in the crack of the window.

  Though he couldn't see much, Top Dollar could see enough of Roc's forehead to put him on a bus to hell. The Hummer sat so high up that Top Dollar had to climb on top of a car to get a better aim. He rested his 9mm on his forearm for a steady shot. Lil Mac couldn't take the sight of losing more of his men as Roc dropped three more, so he thought of another way out and said, "Roc the police are coming."

Roc turned and looked at Lil Mac when four cops entered the parking lot. Right then, a bullet hit Roc's shoulder blade and he dropped his Mack 10. Another bullet grazed his neck before he leaned over near Lil Mac. The head rest blew up into pieces as Roc hit the button to raise the window. Just the movement of his arm shot pain through his body, but the agony didn't affect Roc because his father made sure that he was ready for days like this.

The cops were now getting close, so Roc stepped on the gas and raced into the next level of the parking lot. He hit the back of a parked car when he lost control from driving with one arm. Lil Mac grabbed the steering wheel but Roc never took his foot off of the gas. "Roc you're losing a lot of blood, pull over so I can drive and take you to the hospital," said Lil Mac. Roc pulled over and sat up, turning on his disc player to hear his favorite song by Tupac come through the speakers. He turned to look at his brother and said, "They'll never take me alive Lil Mac." Roc tightened his grip on the steering wheel and then pulled back into traffic. "I guess old head was right…when you hit and miss, you buy something like

164

this." Roc hit the dash board hard on the bullet proof

Hummer.

Chapter 21

Haffee was awake at 5:00 am making, fajr, the Morning Prayer for Muslims. When he finished, he tried to wake Boggy up, "Yo Boggy, get up baby boy. Today's the big day and the C.O. will be here in a half hour. Boggy...Boggy, man get up." The sound of the cell door popping open got Boggy up and his state of mind went straight to war time. Once the door was open, Chris, Bo and a few other inmates came into the cell to see them off.

"What's the deal? Ya'll ready to touch the street and get up out of here?" one of them asked. "I've been ready; it's on when I leave here. I'm not coming back to a cell. I'm going to die on the street like a man, not in a cage like a dog," replied Boggy. "I hear you. That's the way it's supposed to be, but you need to get your stuff ready, the C.O. will be back to get us soon," said Chris. "Ya'll going to court too?" Boggy asked. "Yeah, we're going to your trial. Roc bailed us out this morning. We can't do anything more for you in here. It's time to put that work in for you on the street; you know…two faces one tear." Chris said as he and Boggy did their special handshake.

Haffee walked down the tier to the Iman cell to say his goodbye. "Assalamu Alaikum Iman, may I come in?" Haffee asked. "Yes Haffee, please do come in." "I came to give you this," said Haffee as he handed Iman three hundred books of stamps and five hundred dollars in real cash. In jail, the money was given in books of stamps that were equivalent to six dollars for each book.

Iman looked at him and said, "You don't have to give me anything Haffee. I will be happy if you go out of here and fear Allah. Your heart has life in it. It is well and has illness in it; one of the two will manage to dominate it. Your heart has love for God, faith, sincerity, and reliance upon him. These are what give it life and without this your heart will die. There is also a craving for lust and pleasure so you strive to experience them. It's also full of self admiration, which can lead to its own destruction."

Haffee listened very attentively as Iman continued to share his words of wisdom, "I love you for the sake of Allah and I want the same for you as I do for myself. I want to have a healthy heart. On the day of resurrection, only those who come to Allah with a healthy heart will be saved from the fire. In 26: 88-89 of the Quran Allah said: *the day on which neither wealth nor sons will be of any use, except for whoever brings to Allah a sound heart.* You can find it in the purification of the souls." "Thank you, Assalamu Alaikum," said Haffee. As he thought about everything that Iman said. Boggy walked up on him and said, "It's on, let's go."

Two undercover cops sat across the street from a red and white brick two story house in the suburbs outside of 69th Street. An hour and a half later their suspect came into sight. He kissed his wife and then made his way to his car. The suspect looked up and down the street before jumping into the car and pulling off. The undercover officers dropped a few cars behind the suspect as they watched him closely. The suspect pulled into a Dunkin Donuts store before stopping on one of the city's hottest drug blocks. He was talking to a small hustler called Ali off to the side.

"What you got for me?"

"I don't have anything right now. It's been slow around here lately."

"What you mean it's been slow? What you got in your damn pockets?

The suspect grabbed Ali up and went into his pockets as the two undercover officers watched. "Man, we can bust his ass right here," one of the officers said. "Not now, we got to make sure we take him in at all cost." The suspect pulled off and ran a red light as he talked to himself. "I'm sick of these niggers playing these games, I'm going to start busting a cap in their asses, all of them Roc and Boggy, especially. They think they got it all mapped out. I'm going to put an end to all of this shit or I'm going to die trying."

The suspect ran a stop sign that was blocked by a wild tree. That's when the undercover officers threw the light on the suspect. "What the hell is this?" The suspect found a spot just to his right and pulled into park. The undercover officers approached the suspect with their hands on their guns. One officer on each side of the car, the suspect opened his door and attempted to get out. The undercover officer drew his gun, "Please, sir, stay in the car." The suspect responded, "Do you know who the hell I am?" "I'm only going to tell you once, sir," the officer shouted. "I'm going to have to get your badge for this," replied the suspect as he got back into the car and angrily rolled his window down.

"License and registration please," the officer asked. "I hope you know what the fuck you're doing because I'm going to have you working traffic after this," the suspect said. The officer took the suspect's license and registration and put them in his pocket. "What did you put them in your pocket for? Did you read them?" asked the suspect. "Yes I did, Detective Rayfield." Shamone pulled the passenger door open and his black desert eagle to the side of Rayfield's head and Mohammed pulled Rayfield out of the driver side, throwing him up against the side of the car.

Mohammed patted him down and once he relieved Rayfield of his gun, he handcuffed him. "You have been found guilty of treason, for plotting the assassination of Haffee and Boggy, and for that you must die at the hands of your enemy. So don't think you'll make it to court today but you will see Boggy," said Mohammed. They put Detective Rayfield in the back of their car and pulled off.

Manny and Buff stayed in the background as Roc talked with John Steward and Sam Clinton. They were in the hallway of the court house before the case was to be called. Roc's arm was in a sling and he had a big bandage on his neck. That didn't stop him from playing his part, though. He was dressed in all Ermenegildo Zegna, a dark blue suit with light blue pinstripes and soft black gators. The court room was packed and anybody that was anybody attended for the fallen soldiers. Even Old Head sat in the back and the feds wanted him for over twenty years.

Gizelle and Lil Mac sat three benches behind the defendant table. Gizelle looked beautiful in her white and orange sunflower dress that hid her stomach since she was a few months pregnant. The remaining rows were filled with Yusuf, T.L, Gotti, Meshane, Shorty, L, Mel Money Bags, Flea, Y.G., Mo, Mighty Baby D and Mr. Holmes. A side door opened and Haffee and Boggy came in, being led to the defendants table.

As Haffee and Boggy entered, people in the courtroom went wild. "All rise for the Honorable Judge Beatrice Brake." After the Judge entered, she said "Please be seated. It is to my understanding that we are here for case number 743726, the Common Wealth vs. Johnson and Mayo, am I correct?" Both of the lawyers responded, "Yes your Honor." "The state, are you ready to present your case?" asked Judge Brake.

"Yes and No your Honor"

"What do you mean by yes and no?"

"Your Honor I can move on with my case but my key witness is not here." The state attorney was Zach Thompson. He wore a plain gray suit, white shirt, and black tie and shoes. He was 5'10" tall, 185 lbs. with blond hair and blue eyes.

"Who is this witness?" asked Judge Brake. "Detective Rayfield of the 39th station, your Honor." Hearing this news, Stewart was on his feet saying, "Your Honor, may I please state for the record that my client requested the speedy trial act. This means, and please don't take this as disrespect to your intelligence, I am aware that you know but I think Mr. Thompson here has forgotten that the speedy trial act states that there has to be a trial within 90 days of the preliminary hearing. Detective Rayfield is the officer that found the gun and without his testimony there is no case."

"Your Honor, I ask on behalf of the state that you give us more time to contact Detective Rayfield and not let these thugs back on the street. They are a menace to society." Thompson walked to the defendants table and pointed into the face of Boggy. "This man here is a known killer on the streets of Philadelphia." Stewart was back on his feet for the second time, "I object, your Honor. Neither one of these gentleman here have been convicted of any crime of that manner. I would like nothing more than for this trial to begin to prove to Mr. Thompson and the world that my clients are innocent. As I said, without a case, the court has to dismiss all charges.

People in the courtroom started to scream out, "Let them go you bitch," "I hate you crackers," "When you come outside I'm going to blow your top off." The Judge called for order in the court and slammed down her gavel several times before the court room got quiet. "Mr. Stewart, please keep those people behind you in order or I will clear this court room. I thank you and I have heard from both sides so I will give you my decision after a ten minute recess.

Boggy sat at the table with a pair of gold eye glasses by Burberry, cream color suit jacket with wool and mohair cream trousers. Haffee looked like he was in a G.Q. magazine instead of a trial. The black tailored Louis Vuitton suit and green Giorgio Armani shirt and tie brought out his complexion. He was also wearing a platinum Patek Philippe Geneve watch that added just the right touch.

"Stewart, what you think she is going to do because I got two dates tonight. One with that sexy dark skinned goddess over there named Deja and the other one is with this old man that needs to learn a lesson about keeping his hands to himself," Boggy said smiling at the thought of what he was going to do to Rayfield. "Like I told Roc earlier, without Rayfield they don't have a case. I see his partner Michael over there running in and out of the hallway to use his phone. But I don't think he can find him. I think that the Judge will let you go because if they start the trial I'm going to beat shit down Mr. Thompson's leg," they both laughed.

"All rise." "I just read over the case and I believe that Mr. Stewart is right at this time. The common wealth doesn't have enough evidence to go to trial today but the speedy trial act begins from when the preliminary hearing is heard, not put on the court docket. So by the preliminary being continued twice before it was heard, the date will become the 29th instead of the 20th. The commonwealth still has nine days before the speedy trial act expires so my decision is to give the state those nine days to have Detective Rayfield appear in court. The defendants are to remain in the custody of the Department of Corrections until then."

"Your Honor under the circumstances of this case I believe my client deserves bail. I think this may be the first case in history that two people on a charge of one gun are being held without bail." The Judge replied, "Mr. Stewart, I have been on this bench for twenty years and I've known Mr. Rayfield for ten of them. He has never missed a court appearance." "Maybe he knows my clients are not guilty, so he didn't come today," said Stewart.

"I don't think that's the reason at all. I just pray that he is all right and with that said, the answer is no," Judge Brake stated and hit her gavel dismissing the court. The bailiff rushed over and re-handcuffed Haffee and Boggy. They were being led out of the court when Roc called out to them. Boggy stopped to scan the crowd for Roc when he stopped at a pair of eyes that had been calling him every night as they stole his sleep.

Boggy thought to himself, no it can't be him as he closed his eyes to escape reality. There they were again staring back at him from inside his brain. When Boggy opened his eyes again the pain was now looking him in the face. He couldn't stop looking at Lil Mac as the Bailiff pushed him in the back to make him move. The push brought him back to reality as the court room was clearing out.

Lil Mac understood the feeling that had Boggy off balance because he felt it himself. That's why he never took his eyes off Boggy as he walked with Roc who was a few steps ahead of him. Roc was talking to Manny as they were leaving the court room. Boggy yelled out, "Roc it's him, its Lil Mac…he's Sol…" Boggy didn't have time to finish his words because the bailiff pushed him through the door. Lil Mac smiled and then Roc asked him what Boggy was saying.

"Nothing Roc, he just called to me to say what's up. You're still giving me that ride home, right? I don't know how my car just broke down like that," Lil Mac said. "You already know I will give you a ride," answered Roc. Lil Mac continued to smile as they walked out of the court room hoping that they didn't mess up his plans this time.

Chapter 22

Raja's chest was still a little sore from the shots that Top Dollar slammed into his vest. He couldn't wait for the day of his revenge. Manny, Buff, and Raja had been looking for Top Dollar everyday after Raja got shot and today was no different. The Get Money click wasn't making it easy for them. They had been so low key you would have thought they left the city until they made the mistake of trying to kill Roc.

Manny and Raja rode down 13th Street with Buff and Mohammed following behind in a dark blue Ford Focus. People were moving around everywhere as a dark skinned man ran up to every car in line passing out the work. Manny spoke into his ear piece, "Mohammed, do you see those two shooters on the roof?" "Yeah I'm on them," he replied. "So how do we get around them?" Manny asked. "For one, they walk so far apart from each other. I need to ride through a few more days to put everything together and then I will have a perfect plan."

The dark skinned man was now at Manny's car window and asked, "How many do you need?" "Is this the good stuff because that last shit you sold me a few hours ago was some bull shit," Manny told the man. "You can save all that rap old head. I ain't given you nothing for free. You know we got the best shit in the whole city. So how many do you want?" "Let me get four of them dimes and if they are good I'll be back." "You've been saying that all week old head and you ain't missed a day or an hour for that matter." The man busted out laughing before giving Manny his coke and then ran off to the next car.

Manny pulled the old black Jetta into the next open parking space. They did this at least five times a day, trying to find any weakness that Solo may have left open. Being that this was the Get Money click's head block, security was extra tight. It took Manny and his team four days of buying coke every couple hours just to be allowed to park on the block.

"Man these young boys out here are off the chain. Look at that shit," said Manny as he pointed in the direction where two young guys were pulling a man out of his car through the window. "Tony, do you have my money? Please tell me you got it," Tom said. Tom was

178

the bigger one of the two at 6'1" and 230 lbs. Dame was the other one, standing at 5ft 8 inches tall and the shortest one in the click that worked for Solo on 13th Street. "The way it looks, he don't have your money, Tom," said Dame and then he punched Tony in his left eye as hard as he could.

From the sound of the punch, it was as if he had broken Tony's face. "Damn you…my eye," Tony fell to the ground on his one knee and then Dame threw a wild hang maker that hit Tony in the back of the head. Tony flew face first into the concrete. Tom and Dame worked their construction Timberland boots all over Tony's body. Raja grabbed the door handle and said, "Manny, we got to stop this. They are going to kill him." "Be easy, Robin Hood, we're here to shut this whole thing down and finish these niggas for good," replied Manny. "Yeah you're right, look at that," Raja said as he started out the car.

Mohammed made sure that the shooter on the roof was walking down towards the other end of the block and then he and Buff made their move. They walked smoothly through the crowd until they were right on top of Dame and Tom. Mohammed grabbed Tom by the neck, lifting him off his feet. "What the fuc…" Tom

179

didn't get to finish his words as Mohammed's hand moved swiftly through the air with a Rambo style knife and cut him from ear to ear.

Buff had Dame in a head lock ramming him into a parked car, face first. All of a sudden shots echoed through the air, just missing him by inches. The AK47 slugs put five big holes in the car. Mohammed backed Buff up and returned fire with his 45 automatic. The AK47 that Jason fired from the roof was too powerful, forcing Mohammed to run for cover. Many shots brought light to the night as he crossed the street with guns in both hands aiming at Jason.

"Buff, he's coming down your way in five on the other roof."

"I see him." Buff quickly released Dame and grabbed for his gun. Dame didn't waist a second taking off full speed across the street. Blood was coming down his face making it hard for Dame to see as he slammed into the Jetta. Dame got halfway off the ground when his head popped open. "Allah Akbar," Raja let the Tech 9 fly, following Buff's lead and busting on the man on the right side of the roof. Four shots slammed into the man's side as he tried to run. The impact caused him to fall freely over the edge making a loud smashing sound when he landed on top of a car.

While all this was happening Nay Nay and Top Dollar sat in the basement at a table in one of their many money houses. They had to get the money together because when it came to this aspect of the Get Money click, Solo didn't trust anyone but them. Their key job was to make sure that their weekly numbers matched his. Each person played an important part. D's job was to separate the money by the bills and place them into different stacks. Nay Nay took the stacks that filled the whole table and some off the floor.

She worked the four money machines as if she worked for the Bank of America. Top Dollar was the last person to touch the money before it left the house. He made sure that the hundred dollar bills were wrapped in twenty thousand for each stack, the fifty in ten thousand stacks, and the twenty in five thousand stack. They had been at it for a few hours when the blunt cloud escaped the room.

Right then, the door flew open. Top Dollar looked up as Richard rushed down the basement steps with a rusty 380 in his hand. "Top, they're hitting the block right now," he said. "What? Hell no!" shouted Nay

Nay who was the first person to jump up with her gun in hand. They took the steps two at a time, rushing out of the basement. Top Dollar stopped and looked out the living room window to witness massive gun fire and said, "Nay Nay, I want you and Richard to go out the back and come through the alley in the middle of the block. We need to box them in."

"Fuck that, Top Dollar…it's me and you going out this front door together. D, you go out back with Richard. My damn panties are already wet." Nay Nay didn't wait for an answer, she cocked back her 9mm, opened the door and then came out firing. She covered Top Dollar as he ran down the steps letting bullets fly from his 45 automatic. Nay Nay had come for war and she didn't care if she died today as long as it was for her team

"Buff, watch your back more. Just come out of that house," Manny said as he took aim at Top Dollar's bright colored suit. Buff turned half way around when Nay Nay put two shots in his back. Buff fell back but fought to remain on his feet. He let off three wild shots in Nay Nay's direction. Still firing, Nay Nay moved with the quickness of a cat so that she could get down the steps to hide behind a car next to Top Dollar.

Raja reloaded the tech 9 as he saw Buff fall on top of Jason's body. "Manny cover me, I got to get Buff from being out in the open, "Mohammed said. Manny popped out from beside the row-house and started shooting in every direction. Raja covered also from across the street. Mohammed was once again back in his zone in Iraq. He zig zagged across the street while feeling bullets fly past his head. This made him feel even more at home. Mohammed saw something out of the corner of his eye and dropped to the ground, rolling under a car.

D and Richard stepped out from beside the house firing on Raja and Manny. A shot slammed hard into Raja's vest. "Aaahhh, damn not again," he screamed. Four cop cars came down the block with their lights flashing. The first two cop cars pulled to a stop facing each other and were two cars away from Top Dollar. Nay Nay saw that their doors were open with a cop on each side and they were holding their gun in hand. An officer in the back opened his door and spoke from his speaker, "Freeze, drop your guns and come out with your hands up!"

"Fuck that," Nay Nay said, jumping up from beside the car with a gun now in both of her hands. She fired on the cop and her first shot hit one in the neck and Top Dollar put the other cop down. Raja's tech 9 filled the cop's car on his side with holes, breaking the windows as the cops body lay half on the passenger seat and the rest on the ground. The other cops tried to save their partner but were outnumbered. D and Richard turned their attention to the cops and started firing.

In the mix of the action they never saw Mohammed slide from under the car. Mohammed put his gun to Richard's rib cage and squeezed the trigger. D spun around to be face to face with the 45 automatic. "This is not your war, Sand nigger. Go home, matter of fact I'm going to send you," Mohammed let the bullets fly. "Allah Akbar!" Mohammed pulled Buff's body to the blue Ford Focus, rested him on the back seat as she pulled off. The car took several shots before it stopped beside Manny and Raja. "Come the hell on and get in so we can get the hell out of here," said Mohammed as the back window blew up into pieces. Nay Nay let her gun loose as her air max shoes barely touched the ground running towards the Ford Focus. A shot slid off the roof of the car just missing Manny's head as he disappeared into the car and down the block.

Detective Michael just finished asking Kim three hundred questions about Black's murder again. He was trying to put together the pieces of notes that Rayfield had on his desk and in his locker. The court hearing was in two days and he still hadn't heard anything from his partner. Detective Michael knew there was a connection between the Get Money click, to Roc and Boggy, because it said it all through Rayfield's notes. But he couldn't put his finger on it. "If only you were here to help me," Detective Michael said to himself as he was driving.

Detective Michael was maneuvering through the traffic ten blocks away when the call came over his car radio, "Shots fired on 13th Street, again any car in the location please respond." "This is Detective Michael. I'm en route to the scene." He took off speeding as he went in and out of traffic. Half way there another call came over the radio, "Officer down, I repeat officer down we need back up." Multiple shots could be heard in the background as the officer spoke. "I repeat we need back up, we're pinned in at the far end of 13th Street."

Detective Michael spotted a dark blue Ford Focus racing out of the back of 13th Street. The Focus flew passed Detective Michael doing 110 mph going the opposite direction. Detective Michael turned his head to see three black males in a shot up car with its window out. Making the decision that these men had to be the suspects, he made a U turn, "This is Detective Michael I need you to run this license plate number 34887." A response came back, "That vehicle is stolen." "Roger that. I'm in pursuit of a dark blue Ford Focus speeding down 9th Street. Suspect believed to have been involved in the shootout on 13th Street." Copy that. I'm sending back up."

A shot came crashing through the windshield and the bullet was so close to Detective Michael's head that the wind moved his hair. A second later, a lot of pain went through his body as Raja's second shot made contact with the detective's chest. Detective Michael lost control of the Crown Victorian car that he was driving and raced into the oncoming traffic. He slammed into a black Nissan Altima.

Chapter 23

Roc, Mr. Holmes, and Lil Mac were going deep sea fishing off of Mr. Holmes' 100 foot yacht in upstate New York. The weather was warm, a divine 80 degrees, so Mr. Holmes decided to fly Roc up for another one of their relaxing fishing trips. Roc asked, "What's up with me bringing Lil Mac with me? I think it would be good for him, and you did say that you wanted to talk to him for me about staying out of these streets." Mr. Holmes said, "Please bring Mac, I wouldn't have it any other way."

Now their fishing pole rested in the quiet peaceful water. Three of the eight women crew prepared the dinner table. Roc and Mr. Holmes sat in the soft white leather chairs on the second level of the three level yacht, playing chess. Lil Mac watched with anticipation. The score was two – two and they were playing the best out of five. For 40 g's, the money was just a number for the both of them. The game was about respect of the mind, young against old, though neither one of them would admit it. "Old Head, it's your move," Roc said. "Yeah I know," replied Mr. Holmes as he moved his knight into the lower corner and then said, "Check mate."

Roc couldn't believe Mr. Holmes didn't go for his free queen, instead, he left it for three moves and just pushed down the two pawns. Roc passed the money off then asked, "Why didn't you take the queen like always?" "Because many times the answer to all of our problems is right in front of our faces and we never see it," explained Mr. Holmes. While Roc was still looking at the last chest move, Mr. Holmes stopped talking to look Lil Mac in the eyes. "So, you didn't see the queen move?" asked Roc. "Of course I did, but it was the two moves you would have made after I took it that would have hurt me," said Mr. Holmes as he and Roc started laughing. "Old Head, I'm going to go downstairs and get some rest before dinner," Roc said walking out of the room.

Lil Mac jumped in Roc's chair and started setting up the chess pieces. "You want to play me, Mr. Holmes?" he asked. "I don't know Lil Mac, I have a feeling that you're smarter than all of us," Mr. Holmes replied. Lil Mac smiled and said, "We'll never know that

answer unless we play, after all it's only a game."
"There's nothing you play in life that is only a game,"
Mr. Holmes stated, picking up the white chess pieces and
pushing his pawn into the center space. "It depends on
who you're playing and what you're playing for," Mac
said and then moved his pawn into the center.

Rapidly they both started bringing their pieces
out. Mr. Holmes took the bishop and told Lil Mac,
"Some people should never become an opponent." Lil
Mac said, "But there are times when we are forced into
the game by our surroundings and we don't know our
opponents until five moves are already made." Lil Mac
made a smooth power move, considering his position of
pieces and took the knight. "So after a move is made on
an opponent who should never been an opponent, the
game should be annulled because some people are
irreplaceable and every good chess player sees five
moves ahead...check," said Lil Mac. He moved his king
one space to the left before and continued talking, "Life
is a little like this chess game. See that move you just
made by making me move my kings; I can no longer
castle if I want to. So then I'm forced to make moves that
I might not like, but I can live with them...check." Mr.
Holmes moved out of check.

They moved back and forth for a moment, both players planning their final attack when Mr. Holmes stopped and became silent. Then he said, "I sat here and listened to everything you had to say and that was because you can't understand a person until you know a person. Over the years I've learned that every word that comes out of our mouth could have been a lie and you still would have told me the same story about yourself." "How is that Mr. Holmes?" Getting out of his chair, Mr. Holmes waved for Lil Mac to come follow him as he stopped at the front of the Yacht. Mr. Holmes closed his eyes and took the fresh air deep into his lungs before he continued talking to Lil Mac.

"Your first weakness was how badly you wanted to play the game. Right there you gave me power over you that I wasn't supposed to have and that told me one thing. Secondly, it was the way that you moved your pieces. I could tell that you got part of your game from Roc and the rest you pulled together yourself. But you can't tell the difference from the moves that came from your father." Mr. Holmes walked back and sat in the same chair. "Roc must've let you win a couple of battles. Seeing that you're so competitive, he would have wanted to keep your confidence high, and you took it for weakness and stopped letting him teach you. I know that right now you're asking yourself how I know all this? I'm going to answer your questions because I like you and I love Roc. I don't give people outside of my circle game at this level. The first reason is because you didn't use one move that I taught Roc, which means you don't know any of them, if you did, I would have never gotten your queen that easily. Speaking of that, whose move is it?" "Yours," Lil Mac answered.

Mr. Holmes studied every move possibility once and then said, "Your best defense in life or in chess is when you have all of your people around protecting you, the king. It's like you're invisible but when they find out who the king is then he can be touched. You can then see if he can play on the next level...and by the way, that's check mate." Lil Mac's brain was all over the place. He didn't know what to think or how to take everything that Mr. Holmes said. Then it was the chess game all in itself, Lil Mac considered himself to be one of the best. He felt that he could beat Roc at any time in chess so when he saw that Mr. Holmes struggled to beat Roc, he just knew he was going to win.

In the end, it wasn't so much the fact that he lost that had his mind going, but the way that he lost. Mr.

Holmes let Lil Mac think he was winning the whole time so he would feel relaxed and talkative. Lil Mac was even up two pieces but when he looked up from taking the other knight, Mr. Holmes was waving goodbye. Lil Mac thought to himself, this guy is a clown. There is no way he is going to win this game and then five moves later...check mate. The words were playing in slow motion in his mind, "Every great chess player moves five moves ahead."

Two beautiful women came into the room, "Mr. Holmes, dinner is ready." Lil Mac was still looking at the ways he could have stopped the move when Mr. Holmes touched his shoulder, "Don't worry yourself about that. It happens, now go get ready for dinner." The dinner table was prepared for three people but they had enough food to feed twenty or more. They had everything from deep fried turkey, mashed potatoes, greens, steak, chicken, macaroni, carrot cake, four different kinds of cheese cake. You name it, it was there. The women came to pull out their seats, but Mr. Holmes waved them off.

Lil Mac took his seat and couldn't believe his eyes as he took in everything. He knew that this was the life that he had to live and he wanted it all; from the solid gold and platinum chess pieces, to the yacht with the two swimming pools. The all woman staff that walked around with pretty 9mm's on their hips, the helicopter that sat on the heliport on the yacht, weren't the last or the least on his list. Mr. Holmes noticed Lil Mac's distant look and asked, "Is everything all right, son? You seem like your mind was somewhere else."

When he heard the words, Lil Mac instantly became mad at himself because he knew he had to keep himself on point at all times around Mr. Holmes. It was something about the way Mr. Holmes looked at people, almost as if he was reading a book...your book. "Yeah, more like another world but I will be there soon, you can bet on that," Lil Mac replied and looked passed the gold and crystal chandelier at the most beautiful picture that he'd ever seen. It was painted on the ceiling. "Yeah you can bet on that," Lil Mac said as they began to eat.

They joked around together and all in all it was a lovely dinner. Dessert was ready to be served in the movie room as Dream Girls played on the theater size screen. "Roc, after the movie we can fly into the city to see the Knicks game. I got box seats and I think they're playing the Lakers," Mr. Holmes said. "Don't you own a peace of them?" Roc asked. "No, I turned that down, but ever since that fight with Denver, they have been playing real hard. What do you want to do, grab a piece with me and get this corporate money?" Before Roc could answer, his phone went off and then Lil Mac's phone rang also. They both picked up at the same time.

"Yo what up," said Roc.

"Yo what up," Lil Mac said as if it were an echo.

"When did this happen?" Roc said.

"When did this happen?" Lil Mac again unknowingly repeated Roc's words. Lil Mac looked over the five row seat to where Roc sat and talked on his phone. He had hate in his eyes while he listened to Top Dollar tell him what had taken place just moments ago on 13th Street. Roc had the look of concern on his face for Buff as Manny told him what happened. They both listened to the rest of the story. Simultaneously they both said, "I'll be right there, one," and hung up their phones.

Roc got up and walked over to Mr. Holmes who was now sitting in the center of the theater. He moved to give Roc his privacy when the phone rang. Lil Mac jumped up out of his seat and raced over to where Roc stood with Mr. Holmes and at the same time as Roc said, "Something important just came up and I have to go." Mr. Holmes smiled, looking at them both. Then he walked over to the wall and pushed the button on the intercom. "Jamie, have the helicopter ready in five."

Ten minutes later, Roc and Lil Mac were saying their goodbyes as they boarded the helicopter. "All right, Old Head, it's been lovely as always. Too bad I had to leave this but I'll see you as soon as you get back to the city," Roc said and hugged Mr. Holmes. It was clear that something was wrong and Mr. Holmes looked at Roc and said, "I can see that something is on your mind." "I'm cool old head; it's just that I didn't want to do something because I know what comes with it. But superman is back in the building. So you can save me a piece of the Knicks." Roc jumped on the helicopter. "Thanks for having me Mr. Holmes," Lil Mac said, shook his hand and then went for the helicopter door. Lil Mac turned around and said, "Mr. Holmes, can I ask you something?" "Please do." "How did you know what I was thinking?" "It's in your eyes. They tell a story that you will never tell." Mr. Holmes watched the helicopter move through the air and said to the beautiful woman standing next to him, "Jamie, get Boggy back on the phone now."

Shamone picked Roc up from the heliport in the H3 Hummer. They raced through the city traffic at top speed. Shamone didn't let off the gas until they made it to Roc's hide out in Southwest Philly. The row house was the last one on the block. Shamone grabbed the two green army bags off the back seat, then followed Roc as he ran up the steps and kicked in the front door. The door flew open and they ran in. The back room was just like Roc had left it, one bed, a desk with a lamp on it and the picture of Malcolm X holding an AK47 with the words "By any means necessary" written on it. This room was the most important part of the house.

Roc bought the house for twenty seven thousand, but paid over sixty thousand on this one picture. Shamone ran through the house making sure it was as empty as it looked. He walked in the room with Roc and said, "Its all clear." Roc stepped up to the picture and put his finger on Malcolm's eyes and watched as the fake wall rose up. "Damn Roc, what you going to do kill the whole state?" Shamone said after seeing all the artillery.

Roc stepped inside the wall where there was over 40 AK47's, 30 AR15's, 60 M16's, 100 bullet proof vests, tech 9's, 45 automatics, 9mm's, Rocket propelled bombs, and body bags. "If I have to, I will. Now let's get this shit out of here," Roc said. They filled both bags to the top and there were mad guns left. Roc grabbed one of the bags from out of the wall with two hundred thousand in it for throw away money. As they left and got into the car Roc said, "Call someone to fix the door."

Shamone did the special knock on a basement door as Roc stood in the shadows. Dr. Woods opened the door for them to enter. Manny and Raja sat around Buff's bed listening to their fallen soldier tell jokes, "So we're in the living room, it's me, my Dad and my date…some white chick I brought home. Can't remember her name but anyway, she said that she had to use the bathroom. So she got up and went and as soon as she was out of the room my dad leaned over to me and said, "Son, do you know what the black man's kryptonite is?" I said, "no dad." This nigga said, "Dirty white women and fried chicken." Everyone busted out laughing.

"I see you got enough energy to still tell jokes," said Roc as he walked to Buff's bed side and gave him a handshake and halfway hug the way men do. He continued, "I thought it was a joke when I heard you and the desert storm warrior here turned a basic lookout job into shoot out alley." "You're right, this one is on me. I really don't know how it happened. Mohammed started talking about a fallen soldier and shit, the next thing I know I'm believing that shit. You know how I ride, if it's

197

on then it's on." "That's right soldier, we fight the war until the end or until we pay with our life, no women and children, no retreat."

"I'm glad to hear you say that Mohammed, because I got a plan that will have our names locked next to the game for years to come; passed your grand children's grandchildren. When hustlers speak about the game and they say I remember; best believe our names will come out of somebody's mouth." "Put it on the table Roc, what's the plan?" asked Raja. "Ill tell you in two days. I still need two more key pieces for the plan to be complete, but in the mean time take this." Roc released the bag from his shoulder and dropped the two hundred thousand dollars on the floor.

"That's what I'm talking about, man, make it rain," said Buff as he tried to get up. But the pain in his body was unbearable forcing him to rest his head back on the pillow. "Chill baby boy, you're going got get yours off the top," Manny assured Buff and picked up 50 g's and threw it on Buff's bed. "And you can have the most, but I need you to get better because me and Raja can't do this without you." As Manny talked, a slow tear ran down his face from his left eye for Buff. "Look at me when I'm talking to you, Buff." "Come on Manny you crying and shit, I'm laying in this bed because I jumped the gun and if you and Raja weren't there…"

"Buff, listen to me," said Manny. Buff was now looking Manny straight in the eyes as he was speaking, "this is my word and it doesn't have anything to do with Roc, no disrespect." "None taken" "I'm going to put Top Dollar in the ground and that pretty girl that likes to bust her gun. And I'm going to get anybody that gets in the way." Everybody in the room knew that when Manny gave his word it was like it was written in stone. Roc understood Manny's pain because he felt it also. "Roc, can I do anything to help you put the last two pieces of the plan together?" asked Manny. "Yeah, bring me Rayfield," Roc replied.

Chapter 24

The lights were down and Keith Sweat's music was playing as Deja licked the chocolate and whip cream off Boggy's balls. She moaned as she held one in her mouth and then moved to the other. Deja made sure there was not a drop left as she worked her tongue like a snake up and down the sides of his manhood, savoring the rich taste of smashed strawberries that covered it. As she continued to lick it, she asked Boggy, "Do you like that?" "Do I?" he replied. She put her hot mouth just over the head of his manhood and moved in a circular motion, going up and down while slowly increasing her rhythm taking him deeper into her mouth. Deja used every part of her body for Boggy's satisfaction. Her one hand stroked his manhood as the other massaged his balls.

She squeezed her thighs together putting pressure on her clit and love box to keep it hot for Boggy. Boggy took it as long as he could until he was ready to pop as

Deja worked the length of his manhood in her mouth again. He picked her naked body up into the air and she wrapped her legs around his waist. Sucking on his neck as he carried her down to the bedroom, they didn't make it as he slammed her back up against the wall and slid his dick inside her. "Oh my God it feels so good, baby," she cried out. "Don't baby me now," Boggy said as he pumped away.

From the force he used, it made it look like she was trying to jump over his shoulders. Boggy gripped her soft thighs tightly, took a step back and roughly put her on the rug. He moved the head of his dick up and down on her clit, this made her nipples hard and her love box leaked out her wetness. He sucked on her nipples hard as he plowed his dick back into her hard. She pushed back in ecstasy as the multiple orgasms had Deja's legs shaking and digging her nails into Boggy's back. Boggy loved the pain as well as Deja, so he welcomed it. She sucked on his chest as they continued for ten minutes and then Boggy bent her over at the waist fondling her ass cheeks before spreading them. He ran his dick between the crack and entered her from the back, making her left tit swing while she sucked on her right one.

Feeling himself about to cum, he said, "Whose is this?" "It's yours Boggy…it's all yours, Boggy," she said moaning. Boggy pulled out and came on her back as he said, "It's not mine. It's the game's. It's just the fact that we are the game right now. Niggas do what they can and we do what we want. I'm going to show ya'll today." Boggy stepped out of Deja's condominium into a nice summer day. He pushed the button on his remote to let his top down on his brand new custom BMW 645 convertible. Boggy had the car done by Flex himself with Louis Vuitton interior.

The inside system of the car was changed with a 10" Fahrenheit T.V. screen that flipped down, his PSP and DVD player were self contained in the glove box. They connected to the interior. The shoes were 26 axis with custom black chrome spinteck 'Mask Spinners.' Boggy pushed another button and the engine started. The sound from his four Rockford Fosgate Subs filled the air with 50 Cents' "Many Men." Boggy pushed through North Philly doing 35mph like he owned it, because he did. He rode down one block and then two, stopping to make sure everything was still running the way it should be.

Everywhere Boggy went people showed him love. He stopped at a shoe store to grab several pair of the new Nikes that he missed while he was locked up. A sexy phat caramel woman named Nina moved right in on Boggy when he walked through the door. He picked out fifteen pair and went to pay for it when the owner told him, "Boggy your money is no good here, it's on me. I'm just glad you're home now...stay out." Boggy just smiled and walked out.

Making a right turn down block three to receive more love from everybody who was waving and calling his name, Boggy pulled into a parking space. A voice hollered out of the window, "Yo, you got to move that car, that spot's taken." "I don't see nobody's name on this shit," Boggy said. A face now came with the voice, as he pointed his 45 automatic out the window, "What you say nigga? Oh shit, what's up my nigga," Chris ran down the stairs and gave Boggy the special handshake. "Damn man, what time did you get out and why didn't anybody tell me?" "It had to be on the low because I had this little situation and I had to handle Deja," Boggy said. "You still at it I see. What's good?" "You know that thing I told you that I wanted to take care of when I got out," Boggy asked. "Yeah let's do it," Chris said.

Boggy and Chris walked down that path before, but the last time Bo and Roc were with them. They cut through the yard and came out in the middle block. Boggy stopped to reminisce about how he let it go so far. "Hey Boggy, I think two cats at the end of the block are trying to move some work on the low but I'm not sure," Chris said. "Nigga is you crazy? Ain't nobody in the city got enough heart to sell on this block, where they at?" Boggy and Chris walked to the end of the block and Chris pointed out, "There they go right here." Boggy pulled out his 45 and threw his hoody over his head.

The two hustlers were so busy making sure that nobody came down the block that they never saw Boggy until it was too late. Boggy put his 45 to the back of the man's head, "Turn around slowly so I can see ya'll faces when I kill you." "Don't shoot, it's me." Lil Mac was the first one to turn around and then D did. "What the hell are you doing out here?" Boggy asked. "We're waiting on D's girl," Lil Mac said. "Don't give me that shit. What you got?" Boggy went into Lil Mac's pocket then into D's and came out with two half ounces of coke, 120 bags of Roc, and $2200 in cash.

"Look at this shit. So you're out here grinding?" Boggy couldn't believe his eyes because Roc gave Lil

Mac everything. "Look, I can't tell you what to do because it's your life and I'm not going to tell your brother you're selling drugs because it would kill him. But this here is my life, so don't let me catch you out here again do you understand?" "Yeah," Lil Mac answered. "And as for this money and stuff, it's mine now. Get off my block," Boggy smacked them both in the back of the head before they ran off.

"I should have never let them go." "Let who go?" Chris asked as they walked up the steps and knocked on a green door. A middle aged man with three missing teeth and a dirty Polo shirt that had seen better days opened the door. "Oh my God it's the boss...hey Rosie look, its boss." "Hi baby, when did you get out, Boggy?" Rosie never heard the answer as Boggy unloaded his 45 automatic into her frame and then walked out as quickly as he came. "I got to finish what I started."

Boggy drove for almost an hour outside of the city and pulled up to an all white three story house. Seeing Boggy on the surveillance monitor put a smile on Gizelle's face. She pushed a button to release the gate and ran out to give Boggy a big hug and kiss to let him know that he was really missed. "Girl, you better stop it, you know I just got out. It might pop off up in here,"

Boggy said jokingly. "Boy, you are so silly," Gizelle said. "And you love it, don't you?" Boggy asked. "Yeah I do so please stay out of jail because Roc hasn't been the same since you left his side."

"Has he changed for the better or for the worse?" "He's back to the same old Roc." "Where is he at now?" "They're in the back playing that damn PSP3." Boggy ran up the steps and then stopped to turn around and say, "Gizelle that change is for the better." "Boy go ahead, and keep my baby out of trouble and out of jail," Gizelle replied.

Boggy opened the door on the third floor of the game room in Roc and Gizelle's house. Roc had over thirty arcade games lining the walls. A fifty two inch T.V. hung from the ceiling that they were playing N.B.A 08 on. Boggy walked up on Roc and put him in a head lock. Roc struggled to get out of it, "I'm going to kill you. Oh shit you bit me," said Roc as he flipped Boggy over his shoulder and pulled his fist back, "Boggy!" Roc's face of anger disappeared instantly and was replaced with a smile. He picked Boggy up off the rug and gave him a real hug.

"It's about time you're back. When did you get out?" "6:00 this morning." "You've been out all this time and you're just getting at me?" "You know what they say, always save the best for last." "That's some bull shit, but it's okay. I brought you something, but John said you weren't coming home until tomorrow so I was going to give it to you at the party we're having for you at the club. But there is no time better than now with all the people I love here, me, Gizelle, Lil Mac." "Lil Mac?" Boggy said. Just hearing his name brought back all the sleepless nights he had, thinking about killing the person whose eyes were behind that mask.

"Yeah, he's over there playing the game. I'll be right back I'm going downstairs to get your gift. You're going to love this...I did it real big," Roc said walking out of the room. Just then Lil Mac stood up from his chair and asked, "What's up, Boggy, how does it feel to be out?" "What the fuck you mean? You know what it is." Boggy walked right up to Lil Mac's face and looked him straight in the eyes. Lil Mac stepped back a few feet to put some distance between them before he spoke, "Boggy, what's up with you, why are you coming at me like this?" "You know why." Boggy said, stepping a little closer before he asked his next question, "Do you think you can do it now?" "Do what," Lil Mac asked. "Kill me?" Boggy answered.

With a look of malevolence, Lil Mac smiled and said, "Maybe." Boggy threw a hard right with an over hand left that landed hard on Lil Mac's chin. Lil Mac fell face first onto the soft rug. He pushed himself back up off of the ground and threw the PSP3 as Boggy tried to rush him. The game hit Boggy in the face, cutting him over his right eye. Blood was pouring down his face and he tried to shake away the stars he was seeing from being hit in the head. Lil Mac began swinging a three piece, trying to aim for Boggy's cut but Boggy split two and caught one in the mouth.

Boggy stumbled back a bit attempting to gain his footing and then faked up high with his right hand. Lil Mac went for it; Boggy ducked his head and rushed Lil Mac. He grabbed him by the waist and picked him up, threw him over a row of chairs. Lil Mac's shoulder was now hurt and he slowly got up on his feet again as Boggy quickly approached him. Lil Mac pulled out a switch blade and jumped out at Boggy, just missing his neck by inches.

Roc and Gizelle were in the living room down on the first floor wrapping Boggy's two hundred thousand dollar gift when they heard another hard thump. "Honey, what are they doing up there?" Gizelle asked Roc. The sound of yet another hard thump that seemed as if it shook the house was heard. "I don't know but I'm going to find out," Roc said as he quickly took the elevator that led up to the third floor. Roc couldn't believe his eyes when the elevator door opened. Ten of the arcade games were broken and blood was everywhere. All of that could be replaced but what hurt Roc was the sight of Boggy pointing his 45 automatic at Lil Mac's chest.

Roc gripped his gun and slowly entered into the room. "Oh you want to be a killer pussy? I'm going to send you where I sent the rest of the want to be killers," Boggy said. Lil Mac was now empty handed with a closed eye, holding his side because of the pain from his broken ribs. Standing with his other hand in the air Lil Mac said, "If you're going to kill me then kill me. I've got a team of wolves that will make sure you're dead by morning." "I know Solo....but I'm going to send them on the train to hell right after this one," Boggy replied.

Roc watched as Boggy's finger tightened around the trigger. Roc raised his chrome Mack 10 at Boggy just as Gizelle had entered behind him. "Put the gun down Roc!" He turned to look at her standing in the doorway. As soon as Roc looked away, Boggy pulled the trigger. "Oh my God," Roc opened fired on Boggy. Boggy's

209

body fell to the floor. Roc ran to Lil Mac and told Gizelle to help Boggy.

Gizelle raced over to Boggy as he fought to keep his eyes open. She started shaking him rapidly as she screamed his name, "Boggy...Boggy wake up, Boggy wake up. You have to keep your eyes open. Roc, he's not opening his eyes....oh my Lord please don't let him die!" Gizelle had tears pouring down her face. Roc dialed 911 before wiping down the whole room. He put Boggy's gun and Lil Mac's knife into a safe built on the floor.

"Gizelle, I need you to stop crying and listen to me. When they get here you don't know what happened, you were in bed and heard a noise, this is how it was...you got that," Roc said. "I don't know anything, in bed, was like this...yes I have it," Gizelle replied as she used a part of her shirt to remove her tears. Roc watched the surveillance camera as three police cars and two ambulances stopped at his gate. "Now go downstairs and erase the tape for the past two days and then cut the recorder off. After that you can open the gate," Roc told Gizelle.

On the way to the hospital a million things were going through Boggy's mind as he thought to himself, "I can't believe this nigga shot me after all we've been through…he tried to put me in a box. When we didn't have anyone else to hold us down we had each other. When we had to fight to make a $30 sale, we fought together. Now I tried to kill the head, then the body and you cross me because it's family. I guess you're riding with the other team now Roc. Fuck it you can die with your other brother because Solo must die!" As Boggy lay there, he could hear a voice say, "Dr. Woods, his pulse is rapidly rising back up." "Why wouldn't it, this man is a fighter. Is everything prepared for operation," asked Dr. Woods. "Yes". "All right, you can put him under and I will be ready in a few minutes."

Chapter 25

Only a thin white sheet separated Lil Mac from Boggy as he tried to understand why he was on this cold metal table with people fishing a bullet out of his chest. "He must have known who I was all along for him to just sit there and let Boggy shoot me," Lil Mac silently said to himself. "How could I be that dumb? Then that bitch Gizelle tried to save that nigga after Roc couldn't go along with it and just let him have it. Yeah, you want to help the enemy…okay we're going to have a lot of fun with you before I put you in the ground next to Roc and Boggy. Yes, the king is now out in the open. You'll see if I can play on the next level."

Roc sat in the interrogation room with his two lawyers at the 39th station as Detectives Brian and Phil questioned him. Detective Michael looked on with a cast from his left arm to his neck. The scar on his face caused by the broken glass couldn't hide the hate in his eyes for Roc. "Now let's go over this again from the top."

"Excuse me Detective, we've gone over this several times and my clients' story has remained the same in this sad and unfortunate crime. My client does not know what happened. As he has stated that he was in the basement, when he came upstairs he found the second story door ajar and his best friend and brother were unconscious on the floor. I believe that Mr. Miller has been through enough for one day," stated one of Roc's lawyers Sam Clinton as he stood up and straightened out his suit.

"So if there is anything else you need to know please contact me or my co-council. I am sure you know of him, Ron Happer out of A.C." A detective replied, "If the both of you want to leave then go right ahead, but Roc here needs to answer a few more questions. Like how a person could break into your castle without you knowing and it took us 20 minutes to infiltrate when we were called? Then there is the surveillance tape....yeah, we went through those also and in the last year you may have missed two hours of recording. Now this has happened and your monitor has been off for two whole days, this is bull shit!" "Calm down Phil," said Detective Brian, grabbing Phil's arm while he stood with his face getting red.

"No Brian, this man is a cold blooded killer and the only reason he's still on the street is because of his money. But I swear on life itself, if I find out you had anything to do with Detective Rayfield being missing I'm going to…" You're going to what? Tell me Detective!" Roc was standing face to face with Detective Phil as he spoke through tightened teeth, "Let me tell you something, God forbid I lose everything I love while I have been here for hours listening to your countless questioning." "That's enough lets go Mr. Miller. If you want my client to stay another minute, charge him with something." The two lawyers made their way out the door with Roc being at the rear. Detective Michael's soul called for Roc's demise as he yelled out, "What's that supposed to be a warning?" Roc stopped at the sound of his voice and turned back around and said, "You can take it anyway you want." As he turned half way toward the door Roc called out, "By the way how's the shoulder….ha ha ha." Detective Michael replied, "It's funny. One day you're not going to walk out of here you black nigger and I'm going to make sure of that."

Outside, Manny and Raja embraced Roc before they pulled off in a black Range Rover. "Give it to me straight Manny, what's the deal and don't hold anything back." "First off, Gizelle said she couldn't stay another night in that house." "So she has three more to pick from, so what's her damn problem?" "I don't know but I sent her to Coatesville with my woman in case Boggy tried something." "Try something? Boggy's family, he would never disrespect." "I'm not saying he would Roc, it's just that things aren't looking right. Dr. Woods said once they got the bullet out of Boggy they moved him to a private room with two body guards like you said. But the anesthesia wore off and Boggy started talking crazy saying that Dr. Woods works for the enemy and he was there to finish the job that you started."

"Raja speed this thing up and get me to the hospital. I have to talk to Boggy, he has lost his mind. If I wanted to kill him then the bullet would have went to his head and not the shoulder of his shooting arm. I just didn't want him to kill Lil Mac," Roc explained. "Roc, Boggy's gone." "What?" "I don't know how he did it but two mask men with guns messed up our body guard real bad. Then they put a gun to Dr. Woods' head and forced him to patch Boggy up and before they left, Boggy said to tell you that, "The blood of my brother will now fill the street."

Those words cut through Roc's heart like a power saw. He closed his eyes and remembered the day so clearly when he was 16 and Boggy was 15, it was a hot Saturday and Diamond St. was super packed with pretty girls and hustlers of all kinds. Pick pockets, dope dealers, number runners, you name it they were there. Roc's name was starting to ring bells and a few people didn't like it but that only made Roc hustle harder. "Damn who is that?" "I don't know but they're doing it," was the whisper from the crowd when Roc with Boggy riding shot gun, moved down the block at 3mph. Eric B and Rakim's 'Follow the Leader' played on the radio in Roc's brand new money green Audi 5000 with gold deep dish hammers.

"Look at that lame Popping Tags Shorty, he got to be able to hide that hate better then that Boggy." "Man, fuck them cats, him and Money Man Homes. They think just because they got it on lock that we're not going to eat. They got another thing coming." "Nah, Money Man Holmes is cool." "Then why is he messing with that hater?" "For the same reason he's going to mess with me, because he's a thinker. Yeah Shorty's a sucker and a hater but he gets money so Money Man Homes deals with him and as soon as he stops making money, Money Man Holmes is going to stop dealing with him and it's not because he is not getting the money no more. Holmes isn't like that, it's the fact that Shorty is a sucker."

They laughed exiting the car and dipped up the block to the rest of the hustlers. "That thing right there is cold, young player, real cold." "Thanks E.T. you know how we do." "See that's the problem with you young boys, as soon as you see a few dollars, you run and go buy a car." For the record I have never ran anywhere Shorty and I guess they are really going to be mad when they see Boggy's new cherry red Saab with the top missing, sitting on them BBS's that's around the corner getting waxed." It was as if Roc gave a sign as "Nobody Beats the Biz" rocked the block by Biz Markie and a man drove Boggy's car down with caution, parking it next to Roc's. In the crowd you could hear people yelling out, "Do what you do player...do what you do."

Shorty's face turned red instantly as he gave a head nod to two of his workers that came dipping across the street. "You think you're really the man and the only reason you're allowed out here to see the few dollars that you get is because of what your Pops did for the game." "That's where you're wrong, Shorty. I'm out here because I spilled blood out this bitch as well as lose it." Boggy peeped Shorty's move and slid right beside Roc. Roc knew they were outnumbered and then thought to himself, this is how a star is made in the hood. "Matter of fact, to keep it all the way real…if it wasn't for the respect I have for Mr. Holmes, you wouldn't be eating at all." "What? Did you hear this clown?" Shorty looked into the face of the crowd before continuing, "There's not a nigga in the city that can stop me from getting paper, boy, and I don't like the way you're speaking to me. I think you should apologize."

Roc made eye contact with Mr. Holmes who gave him a slight head nod. That's all that was needed. Roc threw a quick left hook with a right behind it. The impact sent Shorty flying to the ground landing on his back pockets. Roc gripped the chrome 380 from his waist line and got off two shots before one of Shorty's people grabbed him in a bear hug from behind. Boggy sucker punched the other one, damn near knocking him off his feet. Then he picked him up by the waist and back slammed him over a parked car. Roc fought to break free of the big man's powerful arms.

Boggy wrapped his left arm around the man's neck and locked it into his right. The effect of the sleeper made it hard for the man to breathe. Roc broke free, turned around and gave off five shots hitting the man in both legs, "Aaahhhh." "That's only because I like you, slim." Roc stood over Shorty who was still grounded with blood coming out of his chest. Slowly Roc raised his gun to Shorty's head. He locked eyes with Mr. Holmes again, Mr. Holmes shook his head no while stepping up and easily moving the gun down to Roc's side. "Son please, do this for me and I'll make sure Shorty will forget that this ever happened. I will owe you one."

Roc's arm shook and his veins popped out, he brought the gun back to Shorty's head. "Roc you're a hustler just like your father and it's a lot of money out here to be made but you can't get it by sitting in a jail cell. Look around, there's a lot of people out here with no ties to the game and they will tell. You make the call." Mr. Holmes stepped back and sat on a parked car with his arms folded. "Let's ride Boggy." Roc started his car as Boggy fell into the front seat. "What, you don't want to drive that pretty thing?" "Yeah right, after I come from the hospital." Roc looked down at Boggy's leg and it was covered in blood. "Damn, what happened?" "You shot me." A bullet went through the man's left leg which now rested in Boggy's. "Man, I'm sorry, I didn't mean it."

Don't worry about it; as long as it came from you, it's

just the blood of my brother."

Chapter 26

"How much longer, Raja?" Roc asked as his mind came back to the present. "Ten minutes, this traffic is backed up. Something must've happened." Roc laid his head back against the head rest and closed his eyes again. "Roc, do you know why they were fighting?" "I don't even know, once I saw the gun pointed at Lil Mac, I just tried to stop Boggy from doing what he does best but Lil Mac is going to tell me something."

Miles away a cool relaxing breeze passed over Haffee while he was standing on the Atlantic City boardwalk watching the wind blow through his lovely wife Sakara's hair. She took in the beautiful sight of the ocean waves, "Haffee, I love you with everything I am. That's why I'm still here but this worldly life is killing me. While you were gone, the cops came to our home saying that they were going to give you life if you don't help yourself. I don't like the way you live but as your wife I listen and over the years you schooled me well. So

I know that they're never going to give us anything. If they could give it to you, they would have given it already, but I'm tired of them just coming to my home, we don't need this life we…"

"Allah Akbar, Allah Akbar," was the sound of Haffee's ring tone interrupting her as she spoke. Haffee checked the caller I.D. hoping it wasn't anybody important. Not wanting to end Sakara's emotional conversation. "Damn baby, can you give me one minute…I need to answer this. "Yeah, you go ahead." Sakara turned away and walked down the boardwalk as tears ran down her face. "Boggy, what's good," Haffee said answering his phone. "Nothing, this is war time. I can't believe this nigga tried to put my soul in the ground but I got something in store for him and anybody that's with him. So whose side are you on?" "Man, what the hell are you talking about?" Haffee asked.

Boggy told him how he got shot and how he got out of the hospital. "So are you riding with me or is it on, on sight?" "Wait, wait….hold up Boggy. This is Roc we're talking about and that man would die for you." "Well that is what he is going to have to do now. The question is if you're going to go with him. "Listen, let me get back to the city and I'll call you then with my

222

answer." "Nah, I'm going to call you in an hour because my number is changed and Haffee..." "Yeah" "If your answer is no, don't even pick up because there will be no more rap." Boggy hung up in his ear, Haffee looked for Sakara but she was gone. "Damn" Haffee shook his head. "Here we go again," he then dialed a number and the caller answered, "Yeah Roc we need to talk."

"Hello" "Yo, top, quick turn on channel six," Nay Nay screamed in a panic. Top Dollar used his remote to lower the sound of the O'Jays playing softly in the background. He flipped his 50" plasma screen on channel six, "Gun fire, once again in these mean streets of the city. We've seen more bodies in the beginning of the year then the war in Iraq and this is Philadelphia. I'm Molly Weiss and I'll have more coming to you live outside of Temple University Hospital. Right now, if you look to the top right of your screen, we're taking you to some footage of a beautiful white house which belongs to the infamous Odell Miller, allegedly one of the most dangerous men in this city of death. Earlier this evening there was a report of massive gun fire at the residence that left two men wounded later to be brought to this very emergency room. The police stated that they have very little information due to the lack of cooperation from Mr.

Miller. Mr. Miller is believed to have been present at the time of the incident. What makes this story even more mysterious is that two masked men rushed into the emergency room injuring six people and then left with this man." A picture of Boggy flashed across the screen.

"Mr. Vincent Jackson is believed to be Mr. Miller's un-boss. The police are not saying whether Mr. Jackson was abducted or fled to avoid questioning and possible charges. The other victim is Michael Miller, who is Odell Miller's younger brother that has just graduated from a high school in south Philadelphia this summer. Sadly the young man is still in the I.C.U. Excuse me, your name is?" "Detective Brian" "Detective Brian thank you for speaking with us, can you tell the viewers anything more about this violent crime or the condition of Michael Odell," asked Molly the reporter.

"Well Molly, for the most part we can't speak on it because the investigation is still ongoing. I will say that these streets have become a death trap for the young black youth in these lower income communities and it's sad. We need more people to step up and come forward, how many more young kids must die before we decide enough is enough.. Is everyone waiting for Barack Obama to do it or are you going to?" "Excuse me; quick get a close up on him. Mr. Odell," Molly called out. "I knew you wouldn't want to hear what Detective Brian said as he watched the camera crew and Molly race off after Roc.

Roc only made it a few feet away from the jeep before the reporters were all over him. Manny and Raja kept them at bay as Roc brought up the rear. "Mr. Odell is it true that you ordered over 30 murders in the last two months?" "Who me," Roc replied, smiling and then continued to answer, "That's impossible for any person; with the great police force of Philadelphia." "If that is so, then why haven't they closed any of those cases as well as this one yet?" Roc responded, "That's something that you'll have to ask them." "Mr. Odell, D.A. Earl Dash has been quoted as saying that you're responsible for 48% of the drug trade in the tri-state area, would you like to comment on that?"

"I'm a business man with several successful businesses throughout the city of Philadelphia. I employ over three hundred people who have paid Uncle Sam over 1.5 million in taxes last year. So for the record, I don't know anything about any drugs and the next time you see Mr. Dash, ask him if he would be saying this if I was a white business man. Now if you would excuse me

I would like to see my family. Thank you." "You heard the boss now get the hell out of the way," demanded Manny as he pushed the reporter out of the way. "You heard it here first, the alleged most dangerous man in Philadelphia praised the Philadelphia police department and said that they only make accusations of drug trade because he is black. Once again, I'm Molly Weiss for C.V.T.V. that's all for now, have a good evening...back to you, Chuck."

"Hello, hello...Top Dollar, you still there?" "Yeah I'm here." "How long will it take you to get there?" "20 minutes. I'm going out the door now." "Pack heavy Top because as soon as I see Roc, he's a dead man."

Roc's Gucci shoes echoed down the hall of the freshly waxed floor while Dr. Woods brought him up to date on Lil Mac's condition. "Roc after we retrieved the bullet, we found out that it struck a main artery and in the process Lil Mac lost a lot of blood and we believe that was the cause of his coma. Roc's knees became weak as he stood outside Lil Mac's room looking through the window of the door. One lonely tear slowly moved down his face. Dr. Woods put his arm on Roc's shoulder for a show of support.

"Get your hands off of me," Roc said, pushing Dr. Woods with the force of a mad man. The blow sent Dr. Woods crashing to the ground. He looked up and saw that look again in Roc's eyes. "Roc, I understand your pain." "My pain...it runs deep and I'm about to share it with the city." "Manny, get Mohammed and Shamone on the phone. Tell them to find Boggy now," ordered Roc. He stepped into Lil Mac's room and locked the door. Lil Mac was hooked up to all kinds of tubes.

"Lil Mac, I hope you can hear me because I need you to fight for me now. I know I act like I'm a big tough brother that has it all figured out, but I don't. I need you here. When you moved out, I didn't want you to go. To be real, I needed you to stay. You were my reason to let this life go and to see you do better became my will power. Now I'm losing this fight within myself. I hear death calling me again and I'm not the one that's going to die. When I used to be that way it was because I had to be and somewhere along the way my soul fell in love with the feeling of it and that feeling is winning. I need you back, you're my Robin and not only that, I told mommy that everything would be okay and you know that I can't lie to her. After you beat this, I'm going to buy you that brand new Maybach Exelero. I know it may

227

seem like a lot but you're going to need something live to front in on campus."

"I can't believe this nigga is standing here with these fake ass tears like he really cares about me. We're not family. D, Catty, Raw, K.B., Black, Veg, and Danny were my family. Now all I have left is Top Dollar, Nay Nay and whoever else is willing to ride to the end. I'm going to show them the heart of a man. So I don't need you to buy me nothing. When I get out of here, I'm going to make enough money to get my whole team Maybach's but only after we make it rain in blood. If I got to feel pain, then the whole city is going to feel pain, I don't care who gets it. Damn, that was a cold breeze. Someone must have opened a window. Yeah, what you need to do is go on and get the hell out of here because I'm not trying to hear that you're going to shut the city down. Shit, you been laid back too long. I know you don't have it in you any more," Lil Mac laid there with these thoughts in his head.

Roc was still present in the room unsuspecting of the thoughts his comatose brother was having. Lil Mac's mind continued to focus on getting revenge, "I remember all the stories from school and back in our old neighborhood. Don't mess with him, that's Roc's little brother and Roc will kill your whole family and your dog. Roc had to shoot against four cats from the bad land and he killed all of them. No shorty, you can't hit this weed because if Roc finds out that I gave you some, he'll kill me. Hearing story after story about how bad you were like I couldn't be my own person.

Everybody that told me one of those stories was a coward because a real man never rides another man's stack...he makes his own path and learns from his mistakes. I damn sure learned from mine, the next time I get an enemy on the bus to hell, he better fasten his seat belt because he's getting the front seat. I just hope Mr. Holmes was lying when he said the eyes will tell a story we will never tell. Roc, Roc before you go put that blanket on me...Roc its cold"

Roc wiped away his last tears before walking back out into the hall where Manny, Raja and Dr. Woods waited. "Roc, I assure you that we are going to do everything we can for Lil Mac." "I know Doc, and I am sorry for earlier." "There is no need to go there; all that I ask is that you don't do anything crazy. Your brother is going to need you here. "Doc we go way back so I'm going to keep it real because I owe you that much. Make

229

a lot of room and have some hospital beds ready because you're going to need it."

Roc started down the hall. "Manny, have you heard anything from Mohammed yet?" "Yeah he's hot on Boggy's heels. He done took out a few of Boggy's closest workers and found out that the two people with the masks were Chris and Bo. He also said it may take a little time since Boggy is so close to the streets. The hustlers understand they work for you but they've built a love for him, making it easier for him to be mobile, but he'll get him." "He better," Roc replied.

Nay Nay hid in the dark shadow of a corner with her 9mm cocked a hundred feet away from the E.R. exit. Top Dollar was on the opposite side in the cut dressed in all black next to D's deli acting as if he was on the phone in case some one pulled into the parking lot. The 45 automatic he had hidden behind his leg in his free hand came with a silencer but Top Dollar left it in the truck because he wanted to wake up the night when he killed Roc. "Nay Nay, be on point, the vic's in my vision and he should be at the door in 20, 19, 18..." Nay Nay grabbed her other gun from the center of her back. She heard Top Dollar through her ear piece as he continued to count down the seconds, 5, 4, then she said, "Die slow Roc" as her finger tightened on the trigger.

Manny exited the E.R. and looked around. Feeling as if eyes were on him but not seeing anything, he moved for the jeep. Raja stood outside on point while Roc finished up with Dr. Woods. "All right Doc, I'll be here in the morning but if he wakes up at anytime, call me." Roc slid a nice size knot of money into Dr. Woods' pocket and then opened the door.

"I got him Nay Nay, I can get a good shot to the head and he's out of here." "No Top Dollar, he has my baby in there with all kinds of I.V.'s and tubes in his mouth. I need some of the body; all he has to do is move a little more to the left," said Nay Nay. Roc took another step as two nurses raced into the hall, "Dr. Woods, please come quick Mr. Miller just flat lined."

Roc's heart stopped as everything else moved in slow motion for him. He turned around as the exit door blew into hundreds of pieces. Roc never stopped running, even after feeling the glass cuts on the back of his head, neck, and side of his face. "Sir, you can't come in here," a nurse explained as Roc tried to enter Lil Mac's room to see what was happening. Dr. Woods came quickly over to Roc to and said, "Please Roc, let me do what I need to do. You have to wait in the lobby," and Dr. Woods closed the door. Roc could hear the doctor giving instructions to the staff working to save his brother's life, "Clear."

The End…

Stay tuned for the sequel…….

NEGLECTED SOULS
Richard Jeanty

Motherhood and the trials of loving too hard and not enough frame this story...The realism of these characters will bring tears to your spirit as you discover the hero in the villain you never saw coming... Neglected Souls is a gritty, honest and heart stirring story of hope and personal triumph set in the ghettos of Boston.
In Stores!!!

233

Jimmy and Nina continue to feel a void in their lives because they haven't a clue about their genealogical make-up. Jimmy falls victims to a life threatening illness and only the right organ donor can save his life. Will the donor be the bridge to reconnect Jimmy and Nina to their biological family? Will Nina be the strength for her brother in his time of need? Will they ever find out what really happened to their mother?

In Stores!!!

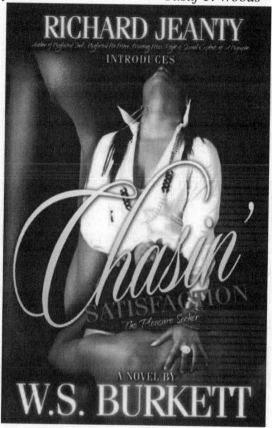

Betrayal, lust, lies, murder, deception, sex and tainted love frame this story... Julian Stevens lacks the ambition and freak ability that Miko looks for in a man, but she married him despite his flaws to spite an ex-boyfriend. When Miko least expects it, the old boyfriend shows up and ready to sweep her off her feet again. Suddenly the grass grows greener on the other side, but Miko is not an easily satisfied woman. She wants to have her cake and eat it too. While Miko's doing her own thing, Julian is determined to become everything Miko ever wanted in a man and more, but will he go to extreme lengths to prove he's worthy of Miko's love? Julian Stevens soon finds out that he's capable of being more than he could ever imagine as he embarks on a journey that will change his life forever.

In Stores!!!

Just when Darren thinks his relationship with Tina is flourishing, there is yet another hurdle on the road hindering their bliss. Tina saw a therapist for months to deal with her sexual addiction, but now Darren is wondering if she was ever treated completely. Darren has not been taking care of home and Tina's frustrated and agrees to a break-up with Darren. Will Darren lose Tina for good? Will Tina ever realize that Darren is the best man for her?

Coming October 2007

Ronald Murphy was a player all his life until he and his best friend, Myles, met the women of their dreams during a brief vacation in South Beach, Florida. Sexual Jeopardy is story of trust, betrayal, forgiveness, friendship and hope.

Coming February 2008

Malcolm is a wealthy virgin who decides to conceal his wealth
From the world until he meets the right woman. His wealthy best
friend, Dexter, hides his wealth from no one. Malcolm struggles to
find love in an environment where vanity and materialism are
rampant, while Dexter is getting more than enough of his share of
women. Malcolm needs develop self-esteem and confidence to meet
the right woman and Dexter's confidence is borderline arrogance.

Will bad boys like Dexter continue to take women for a ride?

Or will nice guys like Malcolm continue to finish last?

In Stores!!!

Tina develops an insatiable sexual appetite very early in life. She only loves her boyfriend, Darren, but he's too far away in college to satisfy her sexual needs.

Tina decides to get buck wild away in college
Will her sexual trysts jeopardize the lives of the men in her life?

In Stores!!!

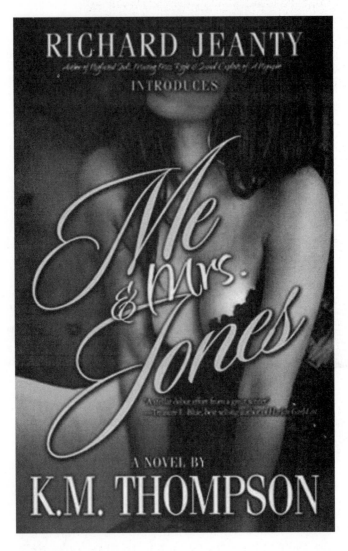

Faith Jones, a woman in her mid-thirties, has given up on ever finding love again until she met her son's best friend, Darius. Faith Jones is walking a thin line of betrayal against her son for the love of Darius. Will Faith allow her emotions to outweigh her common sense?

In Stores!!!

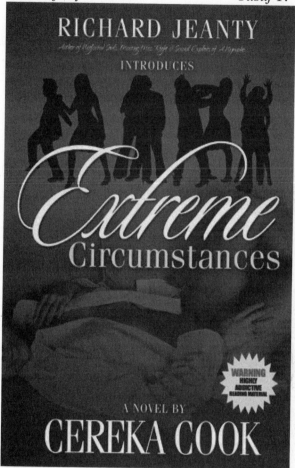

What happens when a devoted woman is betrayed? Come take a ride with Chanel as she takes her boyfriend, Donnell, to circumstances beyond belief after he betrays her trust with his endless infidelities. How long can Chanel's friend, Janai, use her looks to get what she wants from men before it catches up to her? Find out as Janai's gold-digging ways catch up with and she has to face the consequences of her extreme actions.

In Stores!!!

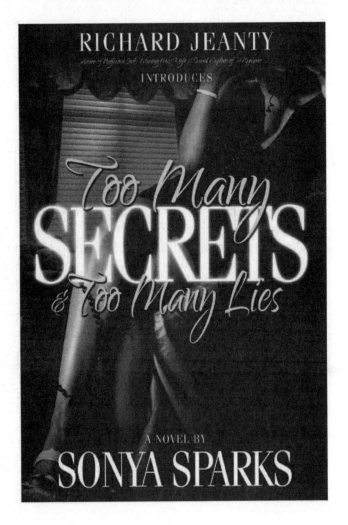

Ashland's mother, Bianca, fights hard to suppress the truth from her daughter because she doesn't want her to marry Jordan who's the grandson of an ex-lover she loathes. In this web of deception, author Sonya Sparks unravels a story that is sure to keep you on a roller coaster ride through the end.

Coming October 2007

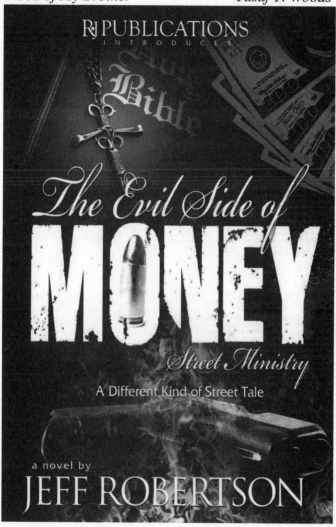

RJ PUBLICATIONS
INTRODUCES

The Evil Side of
MONEY
Street Ministry
A Different Kind of Street Tale

a novel by
JEFF ROBERTSON

Violence, Intimidation and carnage are the order as
Nathan and his brother set out to build the most powerful
drug empires in Chicago. However, when God comes
knocking, Nathan's conscience starts to surface. Will his
haunted criminal past get the best of him?
Coming November 2007

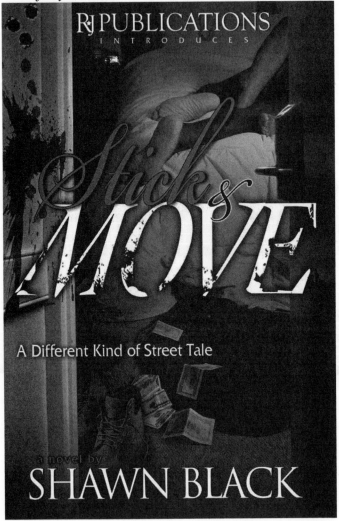

RJ PUBLICATIONS
INTRODUCES

Stick &
MOVE

A Different Kind of Street Tale

a novel by
SHAWN BLACK

Yasmina witnessed the brutal murder of her parents at a young age at the hand of a drug dealer. This event stained her mind and upbringing as a result. Will Yamina's life come full circle with her past? Find out as Yasmina's crew, The Platinum Chicks, set out to make a name for themselves on the street.

Coming September 2007

Also coming soon…

Ignorant Souls
(The final chapter to the Neglected Souls trilogy)
By
Richar Jeanty

Bloob of My Brother II
By
Yusuf and Zoe Woods

Miami Noire
(The sequel to Chasin' Satisfaction)
By
W.S. Burkett

Cater To Her
W.S. Burkett

Kwame
The Street Trilogy
By
Richard Jeanty

Use this coupon to order by mail

1. Neglected Souls (0976927713--$14.95)
2. Neglected No More (09769277--$14.95)
3. Sexual Exploits of Nympho (0976927721--$14.95)
4. Meeting Ms. Right(Whip Appeal) (0976927705-$14.95)
5. Me and Mrs. Jones (097692773X--$14.95)
6. Chasin' Satisfaction (0976927756--$14.95)
7. Extreme Circumstances (0976927764--$14.95)
8. The Most Dangerous Gang In America (0976927799-$15.00)
9. Sexual Exploits of a Nympho II (0976927772--$15.00)
10. Sexual Jeopardy (0976927780--$14.95) Coming 02/08
11. Too Many Secrets, Too Many Lies $15.00 Fall 07
12. Stick And Move ($15.00) Coming October 07
13. Evil Side Of Money ($15.00) Coming 11/07
14. Cater To Her ($15.00) Coming November 2007

Name_____

Address_____

City_____State_____Zip Code_____

Please send the novels that I have circled above.

Shipping and Handling $1.99

Total Number of Books_____

Total Amount Due_____

This offer is subject to change without notice.
Send check or money order (no cash or CODs) to:

RJ Publications
290 Dune Street
Far Rockaway, NY 11691

For more information please call 718-471-2926, or visit
www.rjpublications.com

Please allow 2-3 weeks for delivery.

Use this coupon to order by mail

15. Neglected Souls (0976927713--$14.95)
16. Neglected No More (09769277--$14.95)
17. Sexual Exploits of Nympho (0976927721--$14.95)
18. Meeting Ms. Right(Whip Appeal) (0976927705-$14.95)
19. Me and Mrs. Jones (097692773X--$14.95)
20. Chasin' Satisfaction (0976927756--$14.95)
21. Extreme Circumstances (0976927764--$14.95)
22. The Most Dangerous Gang In America (0976927799-$15.00)
23. Sexual Exploits of a Nympho II (0976927772--$15.00)
24. Sexual Jeopardy (0976927780--$14.95) Coming 02/08
25. Too Many Secrets, Too Many Lies $15.00 Fall 07
26. Stick And Move ($15.00) Coming October 07
27. Evil Side Of Money ($15.00) Coming 11/07
28. Cater To Her ($15.00) Coming November 2007

Name_____
Address_____
City_____State_____Zip Code_____

Please send the novels that I have circled above.

Shipping and Handling $1.99
Total Number of Books_____
Total Amount Due_____

This offer is subject to change without notice.
Send check or money order (no cash or CODs) to:

RJ Publications
290 Dune Street
Far Rockaway, NY 11691

For more information please call 718-471-2926, or visit
www.rjpublications.com

Please allow 2-3 weeks for delivery.

Use this coupon to order by mail

29. Neglected Souls (0976927713--$14.95)
30. Neglected No More (09769277--$14.95)
31. Sexual Exploits of Nympho (0976927721--$14.95)
32. Meeting Ms. Right(Whip Appeal) (0976927705-$14.95)
33. Me and Mrs. Jones (097692773X--$14.95)
34. Chasin' Satisfaction (0976927756--$14.95)
35. Extreme Circumstances (0976927764--$14.95)
36. The Most Dangerous Gang In America (0976927799-$15.00)
37. Sexual Exploits of a Nympho II (0976927772--$15.00)
38. Sexual Jeopardy (0976927780--$14.95) Coming 02/08
39. Too Many Secrets, Too Many Lies $15.00 Fall 07
40. Stick And Move ($15.00) Coming October 07
41. Evil Side Of Money ($15.00) Coming 11/07
42. Cater To Her ($15.00) Coming November 2007

Name_____

Address_____

City_____State_____Zip Code_____

Please send the novels that I have circled above.

Shipping and Handling $1.99
Total Number of Books_____
Total Amount Due_____

This offer is subject to change without notice.
Send check or money order (no cash or CODs) to:

RJ Publications
290 Dune Street
Far Rockaway, NY 11691

For more information please call 718-471-2926, or visit
www.rjpublications.com

Please allow 2-3 weeks for delivery.

PUBLICATIONS
BRINGING EXCITEMENT, FUN AND JOY TO READING

Use this coupon to order by mail

43. Neglected Souls (0976927713--$14.95)
44. Neglected No More (09769277--$14.95)
45. Sexual Exploits of Nympho (0976927721--$14.95)
46. Meeting Ms. Right(Whip Appeal) (0976927705-$14.95)
47. Me and Mrs. Jones (097692773X--$14.95)
48. Chasin' Satisfaction (0976927756--$14.95)
49. Extreme Circumstances (0976927764--$14.95)
50. The Most Dangerous Gang In America (0976927799-$15.00)
51. Sexual Exploits of a Nympho II (0976927772--$15.00)
52. Sexual Jeopardy (0976927780--$14.95) Coming 02/08
53. Too Many Secrets, Too Many Lies $15.00 Fall 07
54. Stick And Move ($15.00) Coming October 07
55. Evil Side Of Money ($15.00) Coming 11/07
56. Cater To Her ($15.00) Coming November 2007

Name_____
Address_____
City_____State_____Zip Code_____

Please send the novels that I have circled above.

Shipping and Handling $1.99
Total Number of Books_____
Total Amount Due_____

This offer is subject to change without notice.
Send check or money order (no cash or CODs) to:

RJ Publications
290 Dune Street
Far Rockaway, NY 11691

For more information please call 718-471-2926, or visit
www.rjpublications.com

Please allow 2-3 weeks for delivery.

PUBLICATIONS
BRINGING EXCITEMENT, FUN AND JOY TO READING

Use this coupon to order by mail

57. Neglected Souls (0976927713--$14.95)
58. Neglected No More (09769277--$14.95)
59. Sexual Exploits of Nympho (0976927721--$14.95)
60. Meeting Ms. Right(Whip Appeal) (0976927705-$14.95)
61. Me and Mrs. Jones (097692773X--$14.95)
62. Chasin' Satisfaction (0976927756--$14.95)
63. Extreme Circumstances (0976927764--$14.95)
64. The Most Dangerous Gang In America (0976927799-$15.00)
65. Sexual Exploits of a Nympho II (0976927772--$15.00)
66. Sexual Jeopardy (0976927780--$14.95) Coming 02/08
67. Too Many Secrets, Too Many Lies $15.00 Fall 07
68. Stick And Move ($15.00) Coming October 07
69. Evil Side Of Money ($15.00) Coming 11/07
70. Cater To Her ($15.00) Coming November 2007

Name_____
Address_____
City_____State_____Zip Code_____

Please send the novels that I have circled above.

Shipping and Handling $1.99
Total Number of Books_____
Total Amount Due_____

This offer is subject to change without notice.
Send check or money order (no cash or CODs) to:

RJ Publications
290 Dune Street
Far Rockaway, NY 11691

For more information please call 718-471-2926, or visit
www.rjpublications.com

Please allow 2-3 weeks for delivery.

PUBLICATIONS
BRINGING EXCITEMENT, FUN AND JOY TO READING

Use this coupon to order by mail

71. Neglected Souls (0976927713--$14.95)
72. Neglected No More (09769277--$14.95)
73. Sexual Exploits of Nympho (0976927721--$14.95)
74. Meeting Ms. Right(Whip Appeal) (0976927705-$14.95)
75. Me and Mrs. Jones (097692773X--$14.95)
76. Chasin' Satisfaction (0976927756--$14.95)
77. Extreme Circumstances (0976927764--$14.95)
78. The Most Dangerous Gang In America (0976927799-$15.00)
79. Sexual Exploits of a Nympho II (0976927772--$15.00)
80. Sexual Jeopardy (0976927780--$14.95) Coming 02/08
81. Too Many Secrets, Too Many Lies $15.00 Fall 07
82. Stick And Move ($15.00) Coming October 07
83. Evil Side Of Money ($15.00) Coming 11/07
84. Cater To Her ($15.00) Coming November 2007

Name_____
Address_____
City_____State_____Zip Code_____

Please send the novels that I have circled above.

Shipping and Handling $1.99
Total Number of Books_____
Total Amount Due_____

This offer is subject to change without notice.
Send check or money order (no cash or CODs) to:

RJ Publications
290 Dune Street
Far Rockaway, NY 11691

For more information please call 718-471-2926, or visit
www.rjpublications.com

Please allow 2-3 weeks for delivery.

Use this coupon to order by mail

85. Neglected Souls (0976927713--$14.95)
86. Neglected No More (09769277--$14.95)
87. Sexual Exploits of Nympho (0976927721--$14.95)
88. Meeting Ms. Right(Whip Appeal) (0976927705-$14.95)
89. Me and Mrs. Jones (097692773X--$14.95)
90. Chasin' Satisfaction (0976927756--$14.95)
91. Extreme Circumstances (0976927764--$14.95)
92. The Most Dangerous Gang In America (0976927799-$15.00)
93. Sexual Exploits of a Nympho II (0976927772--$15.00)
94. Sexual Jeopardy (0976927780--$14.95) Coming 02/08
95. Too Many Secrets, Too Many Lies $15.00 Fall 07
96. Stick And Move ($15.00) Coming October 07
97. Evil Side Of Money ($15.00) Coming 11/07
98. Cater To Her ($15.00) Coming November 2007

Name_____

Address_____

City_____State_____Zip Code_____

Please send the novels that I have circled above.

Shipping and Handling $1.99

Total Number of Books_____

Total Amount Due_____

This offer is subject to change without notice.
Send check or money order (no cash or CODs) to:

RJ Publications
290 Dune Street
Far Rockaway, NY 11691

For more information please call 718-471-2926, or visit
www.rjpublications.com

Please allow 2-3 weeks for delivery.

PUBLICATIONS
BRINGING EXCITEMENT, FUN AND JOY TO READING

Use this coupon to order by mail

99. Neglected Souls (0976927713--$14.95)
100. Neglected No More (09769277--$14.95)
101. Sexual Exploits of Nympho (0976927721--$14.95)
102. Meeting Ms. Right(Whip Appeal) (0976927705-$14.95)
103. Me and Mrs. Jones (097692773X--$14.95)
104. Chasin' Satisfaction (0976927756--$14.95)
105. Extreme Circumstances (0976927764--$14.95)
106. The Most Dangerous Gang In America (0976927799-$15.00)
107. Sexual Exploits of a Nympho II (0976927772--$15.00)
108. Sexual Jeopardy (0976927780--$14.95) Coming 02/08
109. Too Many Secrets, Too Many Lies $15.00 Fall 07
110. Stick And Move ($15.00) Coming October 07
111. Evil Side Of Money ($15.00) Coming 11/07
112. Cater To Her ($15.00) Coming November 2007

Name_____
Address_____
City_____State_____Zip Code_____

Please send the novels that I have circled above.

Shipping and Handling $1.99
Total Number of Books_____
Total Amount Due_____

This offer is subject to change without notice.
Send check or money order (no cash or CODs) to:

RJ Publications
290 Dune Street
Far Rockaway, NY 11691

For more information please call 718-471-2926, or visit
www.rjpublications.com

Please allow 2-3 weeks for delivery.

BRINGING EXCITEMENT, FUN AND JOY TO READING

Use this coupon to order by mail

113.Neglected Souls (0976927713--$14.95)
114.Neglected No More (09769277--$14.95)
115.Sexual Exploits of Nympho (0976927721--$14.95)
116.Meeting Ms. Right(Whip Appeal) (0976927705-$14.95)
117.Me and Mrs. Jones (097692773X--$14.95)
118.Chasin' Satisfaction (0976927756--$14.95)
119.Extreme Circumstances (0976927764--$14.95)
120.The Most Dangerous Gang In America (0976927799-
$15.00)
121.Sexual Exploits of a Nympho II (0976927772--$15.00)
122.Sexual Jeopardy (0976927780--$14.95) Coming 02/08
123.Too Many Secrets, Too Many Lies $15.00 Fall 07
124.Stick And Move ($15.00) Coming October 07
125.Evil Side Of Money ($15.00) Coming 11/07
126.Cater To Her ($15.00) Coming November 2007

Name_____
Address_____
City_____State_____Zip Code_____

Please send the novels that I have circled above.

Shipping and Handling $1.99
Total Number of Books_____
Total Amount Due_____

This offer is subject to change without notice.
Send check or money order (no cash or CODs) to:

RJ Publications
290 Dune Street
Far Rockaway, NY 11691

For more information please call 718-471-2926, or visit
www.rjpublications.com

Please allow 2-3 weeks for delivery.

Blood of My Brother　　　　　　　　*Yusuf T. Woods*

PUBLICATIONS
BRINGING EXCITEMENT, FUN AND JOY TO READING

Use this coupon to order by mail

127. Neglected Souls (0976927713--$14.95)
128. Neglected No More (09769277--$14.95)
129. Sexual Exploits of Nympho (0976927721--$14.95)
130. Meeting Ms. Right(Whip Appeal) (0976927705-$14.95)
131. Me and Mrs. Jones (097692773X--$14.95)
132. Chasin' Satisfaction (0976927756--$14.95)
133. Extreme Circumstances (0976927764--$14.95)
134. The Most Dangerous Gang In America (0976927799-$15.00)
135. Sexual Exploits of a Nympho II (0976927772--$15.00)
136. Sexual Jeopardy (0976927780--$14.95) Coming 02/08
137. Too Many Secrets, Too Many Lies $15.00 Fall 07
138. Stick And Move ($15.00) Coming October 07
139. Evil Side Of Money ($15.00) Coming 11/07
140. Cater To Her ($15.00) Coming November 2007

Name_____
Address_____
City_____State_____Zip Code_____

Please send the novels that I have circled above.

Shipping and Handling $1.99
Total Number of Books_____
Total Amount Due_____

This offer is subject to change without notice.
Send check or money order (no cash or CODs) to:

RJ Publications
290 Dune Street
Far Rockaway, NY 11691

For more information please call 718-471-2926, or visit
www.rjpublications.com

Please allow 2-3 weeks for delivery

Use this coupon to order by mail

141. Neglected Souls (0976927713--$14.95)
142. Neglected No More (09769277--$14.95)
143. Sexual Exploits of Nympho (0976927721--$14.95)
144. Meeting Ms. Right(Whip Appeal) (0976927705-$14.95)
145. Me and Mrs. Jones (097692773X--$14.95)
146. Chasin' Satisfaction (0976927756--$14.95)
147. Extreme Circumstances (0976927764--$14.95)
148. The Most Dangerous Gang In America (0976927799-
      $15.00)
149. Sexual Exploits of a Nympho II (0976927772--$15.00)
150. Sexual Jeopardy (0976927780--$14.95) Coming 02/08
151. Too Many Secrets, Too Many Lies $15.00 Fall 07
152. Stick And Move ($15.00) Coming October 07
153. Evil Side Of Money ($15.00) Coming 11/07
154. Cater To Her ($15.00) Coming November 2007

Name_____
Address_____
City_____State_____Zip Code_____

Please send the novels that I have circled above.

Shipping and Handling $1.99
Total Number of Books_____
Total Amount Due_____

This offer is subject to change without notice.
Send check or money order (no cash or CODs) to:

RJ Publications
290 Dune Street
Far Rockaway, NY 11691

For more information please call 718-471-2926, or visit
www.rjpublications.com

Please allow 2-3 weeks for delivery

256